SEEKING
SPIRITS

DON'T MISS JASON AND GRANT'S

FIRST COLLECTION

OF GHOSTLY ADVENTURES...

Ghost Hunting
True Stories of Unexplained Phenomena from
The Atlantic Paranormal Society

Jason Hawes and Grant Wilson
with Michael Jan Friedman

Available from Pocket Books!

SEEKING
SPIRITS

The Lost Cases
of The Atlantic Paranormal Society

JASON HAWES AND GRANT WILSON
WITH MICHAEL JAN FRIEDMAN

Pocket Books

New York London Toronto Sydney

Pocket Books
A Division of Simon & Schuster, Inc.
1230 Avenue of the Americas
New York, NY 10020

First Pocket Books trade paperback edition September 2009.

POCKET and colophon are registered trademarks of
Simon & Schuster, Inc.

For information about special discounts for bulk purchases,
please contact Simon & Schuster Special Sales at 1-866-506-1949
or business@simonandschuster.com.

The Simon & Schuster Speakers Bureau can bring authors to your
live event. For more information or to book an event contact the
Simon & Schuster Speakers Bureau at 1-866-248-3049 or visit our
website at www.simonspeakers.com.

Manufactured in the United States of America

10 9 8 7 6 5 4 3 2 1

Library of Congress Cataloging-in-Publication Data

Hawes, Jason
    Seeking spirits / by Jason Hawes and Grant Wilson with Michael Jan
Friedman.—1st Pocket Books trade pbk. ed.
        p.   cm.
    1. Ghosts. 2. Parapsychology. 3. Atlantic Paranormal Society.
I. Wilson, Grant. II. Friedman, Michael Jan. III. Atlantic Paranormal
Society. IV. Title.
BF1461.S378   2009
133.1—dc22
                                                        2009025000

ISBN 978-1-4391-0115-5
ISBN 978-1-4391-5539-4 (ebook)

I dedicate this book and all of my work firstly to my wife, Kristen, who has given me the strength when I was down to stand on my feet again. I love you not just as my wife but as my best friend since the seventh grade.

Secondly, I dedicate this book to all five of my children, who have endured their father's passion and allowed me the time to do everything I have accomplished. You all keep me young and have showed me how important every moment we spend together is. Our time together is priceless.

Last and not least, I dedicate this book to every T.A.P.S. family and non-T.A.P.S. family paranormal investigator out there. Your work has helped push this field into a respectable position. Your support is what has made us a success.

—Jason Hawes

I dedicate this book to the hundreds of thousands of paranormal investigators who work tirelessly, dedicating countless hours, hard earned money, and much needed sleep in order to help those who are afraid in their own homes, and to those who are blazing new trails in the field despite pathetic ridicule and seemingly insurmountable obstacles. Thank you for your hard work.

And, of course, to my loving wife and children, ever-present and unwavering in their crescendoing love, support, and importance in my life.

—Grant Wilson

Authors' Note

Paranormal activity is not supported by conventional scientists or by specialized equipment manufacturers, nor can it be re-created in a controlled setting. Therefore the field of paranormal investigation is populated by theory, speculation, and opinion. Due to these limitations, what is shared within these pages is what T.A.P.S. as an organization feels is closest to the truth. T.A.P.S. is not claiming these beliefs to be fact; rather, they are presented as educated theories and observations based on years of experience and research.

Contents

Introduction: Grant Wilson

G host hunting, like a lot of other things we human beings do, has gotten a lot more sophisticated over the years, a lot more technological in nature, and a lot more demanding. If you're going to conduct a paranormal investigation in a professional manner, you need to be savvy in any number of specialized applications. That's why it makes sense for you to have access to a team of experts.

When you see Jason and me on television these days, we've usually got a fair-sized crew working with us. It's a darned capable crew, too. You know them because you've seen them as often as you've seen Jason and me.

On *Ghost Hunters,* these people are fielding calls from prospective clients, loading up vehicles, and driving from one end of the country to the other. They're interviewing, setting up our equipment, and serving as our eyes and ears in various aspects of our investigations. They're packing up in the morning, spending long hours reviewing audio and video data, and conducting research in local libraries, town halls, and historical societies. And when the investigation's over, they're filing away the evidence we've collected so it's available for future reference.

But it wasn't always that way. Back in the day, when T.A.P.S. was just getting started, Jason and I did a lot of that stuff on our own. We didn't have a big organization to fall back on. We were just two guys with a passion for ghost-hunting and a naïve notion that we could help people in trouble.

Sure, we had some welcome assistance. We were seldom left completely to our own devices. But it was often just the two of us, relying only on ourselves and on each other, because there was no one else we could drag out of bed on a Saturday morning to make a six-hour drive up to Maine.

After all, paranormal investigation isn't just a hobby, though we know there are people who look at it that way. It's a responsibility, and a big one. When you're a ghost hunter, you're dealing with people's lives. You're entering their homes, listening to their most closely guarded secrets, going through their personal possessions, and maybe offering them a sliver of hope.

They might not place much faith in their clergy, their doctors, or their local police force. They might not feel comfortable confiding in their friends, their neighbors, or even the other members of their family. But for some reason, they feel comfortable placing their faith in *you*. If that's not a responsibility, I don't know what is.

One of the reasons people depend on us, I think, is that we've been where they are. We've had our close encounters with the supernatural, been scared half to death by them, and been lucky enough to come out whole and sane. So when we sit down to talk with a woman who sees things other people don't see, or a man who hears voices late at night, we can appreciate their confusion and their pain.

We can *identify*.

If you read our first book, *Ghost Hunting,* you know how Jason first came into contact with the supernatural. At the tender age of twenty, he got involved with a woman who practiced Reiki, a Japanese relaxation technique that depends on the manipulation of a person's life-force energy. After six months of exposure to the technique, he started seeing things—including full-body human apparitions.

He thought he was losing his mind. Then he was introduced to a paranormal researcher named John Zaffis, who told him he was just becoming sensitive to paranormal phenomena. That settled Jason's mind, but he was still seeing things everywhere he went. It wasn't until he ran into a stranger at an aquarium—a woman who suggested that he try eating green olives—that he obtained any relief from his visions.

Olives. Go figure.

In the meantime, Jason had founded R.I.P.S.—the Rhode Island Paranormal Society—a support group for people like him, who had had an encounter with the paranormal and felt the need to talk about it. It was through R.I.P.S. that Jason and I met. I was looking to establish some credentials in the field of website design, came across the R.I.P.S. website, and knew I could improve it a couple of hundred percent.

I contacted Jason and discovered that he was interested

in improving the site, and could use the help. A short time later, we met at a doughnut shop and started batting around ideas. But the conversation kept drifting away from websites and toward the paranormal.

We had that interest in common, and we talked about it not only on that night but on many others as well. However, it wasn't until years later, after we had become as close as brothers, that I finally confided in Jason what had happened to me. Because, you see, he wasn't the only one who'd had an experience he couldn't explain. And here, more or less, is the story I told him . . .

I grew up in a densely wooded part of Rhode Island, the paranormal being the furthest thing from my mind. It came up in the form of Halloween and ghost stories, and that was about it. Besides, I wasn't the kind of kid who liked to explore dark, drafty attics and cold, cobwebbed basements, looking for the spirits of the departed. I spent all my free time outdoors, which was why I joined the Boy Scouts and then later on the Eagle Scouts. If you blindfolded me and put me in the woods in those days, I had no trouble finding my way home.

I have a very close friend whom I've known since I was five years old, whose name is Chris. One day, when I was fifteen, we were hanging out in the woods near Chris's house, climbing trees and doing the kind of stuff we always did in the woods. Suddenly, we got an odd feeling that we should probably go home. I can't tell you where it came from, but we both felt it.

It was then that I noticed something moving among the trees. It wasn't an animal, or anything even vaguely resembling an animal, and it certainly wasn't a human being.

It was some kind of distortion in the air, weaving its way through the branches.

I pointed it out to Chris, expecting that he would see it, too. To my surprise, he didn't. He could see the effect the thing had on the tree branches, moving them aside as it went, but not the thing itself. After about a half hour of this, the phenomenon left us, and we stood there bewildered.

"What was that?" I asked.

Neither of us had an answer.

Of course, we went back to that spot the next day, and the day after that, and many times thereafter. Every time, something happened that we couldn't explain. It was scary in a way because we were dealing with something way outside the realm of our experience. But we never felt that we were in danger. Whatever we had stumbled on, it didn't seem like it was out to hurt us.

Finally, the presence revealed itself—but only to me. Chris could see the results of its actions—the dust, the moving branches, and so on—but not the thing that had moved them. For some reason I didn't understand, I was the only one who could catch even a glimpse of our strange companion.

What did it look like? It was short and dark. And from all appearances, very, very curious. In fact, it seemed to want to know about *us* every bit as much as we wanted to know about *it*. It wasn't what you would call friendly. But then, it wasn't shy or nasty or frightened either. It was just . . . fascinated with us.

I looked the thing up in every book I could find, but I still couldn't figure out what it might be. I remember being afraid that it would go away and we would never know what we had discovered. But it didn't go anywhere. Every time we returned to the woods, it was there, waiting for us.

We were able to interact with this thing—this entity— quite regularly over the course of the next two years. It occurred to us that we should run some tests to verify its existence, to prove, if only to ourselves, that we weren't crazy. In particular, since I was the only one who could see the entity, to prove that *I* wasn't crazy.

One day the entity decided to mimic my friend Chris. Once I realized what it was doing, I saw my chance to conduct a test. First I stood between Chris and the sun, so I couldn't catch a glimpse of Chris's shadow and spoil the experiment. Then I asked Chris to stand behind me and make a series of unusual gestures, gestures I had never seen him make before.

I couldn't see Chris, but I could see the entity as it imitated him. Watching it carefully, I described to my friend what I was seeing. Then I asked Chris to tell me if he was doing the same thing.

He was. *Exactly.*

We kept at it for about an hour, and I managed to describe Chris's gestures—no matter how elaborate they got—without a single error. The entity then headed back into the woods. Once again, we were left dumbfounded that such a thing existed, albeit a little more confident that we weren't out of our minds.

We later found that we could ask the entity to be in certain places at certain times—and I'm not just talking about places in the woods. It would show up in town as well. And each time we asked it to show up at a certain location, we would hear of some evidence that it had been there. Not that it had been spotted—I was the only one who could see it—but that something had occurred that wouldn't have happened if the entity hadn't been there.

For example, one time we asked it to be on my friend's school bus in the morning. When my friend got on the bus the next day, which was a Monday, everyone was sitting in the front half of the vehicle rather than the back, even though the back of the bus was where most kids liked to gather. On Tuesday morning, after the entity was gone, a bunch of kids were seated in the back again.

We conducted similar tests on several different occasions. Each time, the entity's presence caused a change in people's behavior. No one saw it, but they reacted to it all the same.

It all ended when I went away to college. The entity remained in the woods, as far as I knew. Of course, I missed it. Because I was the only one who could see it, I had felt a certain bond with it. But there were other things happening in my life. They distracted me from thinking a lot about the short, dark thing in the woods.

Then, as luck would have it, I moved back to the area where I grew up. Of course, I had never stopped thinking about the entity, wondering if it still visited the spot where I first encountered it. Believe me, I wouldn't have been surprised if it decided not to appear again.

I went back to the old spot several times and walked around for a while. If nothing happened, I thought, so be it. But I wasn't there more than a few minutes before I saw something moving through the trees. And as I watched, amazed, the entity appeared again.

As before, I could see it. I could communicate with it.

And it was still curious enough about human beings to renew our relationship, which I still prize to this day.

Is it a ghost? A demon? I have my own reasons for saying "no" in answer to these questions. I have consulted with many so-called experts in the paranormal about my encounters with the entity in the woods, and none of them pretend to have an idea what it could be.

I have spent my life, since the age of fifteen, trying to explain or even just categorize what I have experienced. All I can tell you is that it has been a wonderful part of my life. Far from being frightened or freaked out by it, I feel profoundly grateful for it.

Of course, what I've described here is only the tip of the proverbial iceberg. There are many more parts to the story. But those are for another day . . . if I decide it's a good idea to discuss them at all.

You see, this is the first time I've spoken publicly about my first experiences with the paranormal. Until now, I've kept mum on the subject. No doubt, you're asking yourself why I remained silent for so long.

For one thing, I've always considered my personal experiences just that—*personal*. In other words, a matter between me and the small, dedicated group of friends who saw me through those times. For another thing, I didn't want anyone to think I was just trying to get attention. If you know me, you know attention is the *last* thing I want. I would much rather stand on the sidelines than in the limelight.

Finally, I couldn't stand the idea that people would try to pick apart what happened to me. It was difficult enough to deal with the reality of my encounters. I didn't need the additional burden of trying to prove their authenticity.

Even now, I feel a little uncomfortable talking about it. But for better or worse, it's out there. You decide if you want to believe it.

Anyway, that's how it all began for me. You know where it wound up—with our starting T.A.P.S., also known as The Atlantic Paranormal Society, and crawling on our hands and knees through places most people would prefer to avoid, in search of things few people want to know about. And maybe because we're crazy by nature, loving every minute of it.

Even the scary parts. Or maybe I should say *especially* the scary parts.

Like when a table scrapes its way across the floor for no good reason, or when you're playing back an audio recording and you hear a whisper warning you to "get out," or when you see a human-looking shadow gather in the corner of a room and you know there's no one there to cast it. Or maybe you record a sudden drop in temperature as if all the heat is being sucked out of the room, or you feel something heavy sitting on your chest, and you can't begin to explain what's happening in terms of normal, everyday physics.

Jason and I have had a lifetime's worth of those moments. And, of course, only some of them took place after we started appearing on television. We conducted many of our most bizarre investigations long before we had any idea there would be a *Ghost Hunters* program on Syfy.

You read about some of those cases in *Ghost Hunting*. For instance, the investigation in which a family was visited by apparitions without legs. Or the one in which I was attacked by an angry spirit in a barn. Or the one in which a church was haunted by the ghosts of Civil War soldiers. Those stories struck a chord with you, and you told us you wanted to hear more of them.

That's why we put together this second volume of our adventures as paranormal investigators. Because our television investigations, exciting and intriguing as they may be, can only give you part of the story. The remainder of it is composed of the untold cases that follow.

As you read them, remember—back then we weren't as experienced in the paranormal field as we are now. A lot of times we were feeling our way around and hoping for the best. But then, everybody's got to start somewhere . . .

The Cases:
Jason Hawes
and Grant Wilson

Jason: Playmate

1994

From the beginning of our careers as ghost hunters, Grant and I saw plenty of cases in which a child was influenced by a supernatural entity who had assumed the guise of an invisible friend. But we wondered if the opposite could be true. Could an entity be influenced to some extent by a child?

In the summer of 1994, we were contacted by Alex and Leslie Creighton, a young couple with a four-year-old daughter named Mandy. For the last six months, the family had been living in a rural part of Leominster, Massachusetts. For most of that time, Alex had been victimized by an unseen force.

He would feel blows to his body and painful scratching sensations, as if he were being raked by a sharp set of claws. His wife said she hadn't been attacked at all, nor had she been present during the assaults on her husband. Their biggest fear, of course, wasn't for themselves but for their daughter.

Both parents had seen and heard Mandy talking to someone who wasn't there. At such times, Mandy's voice was calm and steady, and there was no sign of fear in her expression. She was no more anxious at those times than if she were playing with the kid next door.

At first, the Creightons hadn't thought anything of their daughter's invisible companion. But as the attacks on Alex continued, they grew more and more wary. Finally, they decided to engage the services of T.A.P.S.

Grant and I investigated the house for three days straight. We deployed video cameras, audio recorders, and the rest of the equipment we used on a regular basis. Much to the chagrin of the homeowners, we weren't able to catch anything we could even remotely call evidence. However, we did witness an incident while we were there.

At nine-twenty on Saturday morning, while Grant and I were in the kitchen talking with Leslie, Alex emerged from the shower in the upstairs bathroom and started to get dressed. Suddenly, he called out. We charged upstairs as quickly as we could, only to see Alex point to the lower part of his back.

He had four long, angry red marks leading down toward his waist. Just as he was showing us the marks, he was attacked again on the back of his left arm. As we watched, four scratch marks appeared, each one breaking the surface of the skin and squeezing out tiny drops of blood.

Clearly, Alex's complaints had some credibility. Since Mandy's invisible friend was the only other activity reported by the Creightons, we decided to see if we could find a link between the two. To accomplish that, we had to speak with Mandy.

She was a shy child, not especially comfortable conversing with adults. Grant and I had to earn her trust first, playing dolls with her and offering her some ice cream. Finally, she opened up enough to talk about her unseen companion.

We got her to tell us that she had a friend named Tara who would get mad at Alex sometimes. "When does Tara get mad?" I asked her. "When my dad punishes me," said the little girl.

In other words, whenever Alex disciplined Mandy, Tara would retaliate. In the gentlest terms possible, we explained to Mandy that Tara's response was hurting Alex. "And we don't want your dad to get hurt," I said, "do we?"

Once Mandy realized what was happening to her father, she got upset—more so, in fact, than we had anticipated. She told us with a lump in her throat that she didn't want Tara to hurt her father anymore. Though she didn't say so, it seemed clear to us that she would speak to her friend about it.

From that time on, Alex suffered no more attacks. But when we last spoke with the family, which was just a few years ago, Mandy was still talking with her invisible friend. What did she say to Tara, back in 1994, to make her stop hurting Alex? We still don't know. But we learned that, in at least some cases, children can influence the spirits who communicate with them.

Grant: Empty Nest

1994

We've all heard of black cats and the superstitions involving them. For example, if a black cat crosses your path, you're supposed to be in for a run of bad luck. But what about a *white* cat?

We ran into just that question in Norfolk, Virginia, at the home of Robert and Louise Platt. The couple, whose two children were both away at college, were true empty-nesters. They didn't even have a goldfish.

Yet their three-bedroom ranch, from what they told us, was full of activity. At least once a week, they woke up in the morning to find that their living room furniture had been rearranged. They were at a loss to say how or by whom, considering their doors were locked and they hadn't heard any noise.

Sometimes they opened their eyes in the middle of the

night to see vaguely human figures floating over their bed. When they made a noise or a sudden movement, the apparition disappeared. But it left them unable to go back to sleep.

At other times, they heard footsteps approaching their bedroom from elsewhere in the house. But no one ever entered. And when Robert got up to search the house for intruders, he never found any.

They weren't even spared during the day. Both of them heard voices in other rooms. Yet when they went to investigate they found no one there, and no television or radio activity that might explain what they had heard.

Robert had doors slammed in his face on several occasions. What's more, it was never the same door twice, so he couldn't avoid it. It had gotten to the point where he hesitated every time he walked through a doorway.

Louise had always done the laundry in the basement without incident. But lately she had started hearing voices down there telling her to get out of the house. As a result, she was avoiding going down to the basement, and had begun visiting a local laundromat.

Jason and I took Ed Gaines and Brittney Selden, a couple of our most trusted investigators, along with us on this case. It was gray and overcast when we arrived, but not at all cold out. In fact, it was shirtsleeves weather, unusual for late fall.

From the moment we entered the house, all four of us felt a strange heaviness in the air. It was even difficult to breathe. While Ed and Brittney positioned audio and video recording devices in strategic spots, Jason and I sat down and talked with the homeowners.

They were rattled by everything that had gone on, and desperately wanted a respite from what they believed were supernatural events. We explained to them that we would do everything in our power to help them. However, before we could do so, we had to determine if their experiences were in fact supernatural in origin.

Sometimes, as a paranormal investigator, you want so much to help your clients that you buy into their theories hook, line, and sinker. We had to be careful to avoid that. If we were going to help these people, we had to base our recommendations on scientifically obtained evidence, not just on our personal feelings.

We set up our equipment and waited to see what would happen. Hours later, Jason and I were walking around upstairs when we caught a glimpse of something dark—like a shadow. But it wasn't attached to an object, the way a real shadow would be. It was moving into one of the bedrooms of its own accord.

Giving chase, we swung into the room and looked around. And there it was, next to the bed, almost as if it were hiding. For just a second, we got a good look at it. It was a few feet in height, hovering just above the floor. If it had any distinguishable features we couldn't see them. It was too dark and dense-looking.

Then, just as we were thinking we might have cornered it, it backed up in the direction of the wall—and disappeared. We felt cheated. It's not often you get a chance to chase down a visible manifestation of the supernatural, but we had done just that. And now it had vanished on us.

Still, we now had a reason to believe the Platts' accounts. It was a start. As Jason and I were jotting down our observations, intending to add them to whatever audio or video evidence we could record, we caught a glimpse of something out in the hallway.

It wasn't the dark mass—far from it. It looked like an animal, even though the Platts had said they didn't keep pets in the house. And not just any animal—Jason and I agreed on that right off the bat.

As far as we could tell, it was a white cat.

Of course, we didn't just stand there as we arrived at that conclusion. We did it on the run, darting out of the Platts' bedroom. We emerged into the hallway just in time to see the small, white figure slip into one of the other rooms, the one that belonged to the Platts' elder son, Nicholas.

For the second time in the last few minutes, we believed we had cornered our prey. But there was no sign of the cat, if that's what it was, in the bedroom. We looked pretty thoroughly, too, before we decided that it had given us the slip.

We left the bedroom and were barely out in the hall when, to our surprise, we caught sight of the cat again. This time it was scampering into the other son's bedroom.

Again, we gave chase. And again, it eluded us. But having seen the white cat twice, we were even more certain of what it was we had been chasing.

Neither the Platts nor our team had any more experiences that night. In the morning, we collected our equipment, thanked the homeowners for their hospitality, and said that we would be in touch with them as soon as we had a chance to review the data. Jason and I hoped that we had collected some hard evidence, because we had eyeballed some pretty impressive phenomena.

Back in Rhode Island, our team spent hours poring over audio- and videotapes, paying special attention to the times when Jason and I had encountered the dark mass and then the white cat. Sometimes we come back from an investigation chock full of personal experiences and, sadly, find nothing in our data to confirm them. This time we were more fortunate.

Our video recordings showed us a great deal of globule activity in the home—in other words, the presence of balls of light that seemed unrelated to any other source of illumination. It was particularly noticeable in the bedrooms, the hallway, and the basement, where the Platts had reported seeing or hearing ghostly events.

Even more important, we managed to record several discernible EVPs at the Platt house, some of them echoing what Louise had heard down in the basement. EVPs are electronic voice phenomena, or words and phrases that can be picked up only by an electronic recording device and not by the human ear. Sometimes, EVPs can be made more understandable through the use of a sophisticated editing system, which we used in this instance. Unfortunately, it wasn't as helpful as we had hoped. In the end, we had what we had, which was still sufficient for us to say that we had indeed encountered paranormal activity.

We called the Platts and informed them of our findings. Despite the doors that had slammed in Robert's face and the aggressive tone of the voices that addressed Louise in the basement, we concluded that the spirit behind all the activity was a human one—the disembodied remnant of what had once been a human being, and not a demonic entity. More than likely, this spirit was a previous resident.

And it was just trying to scare them out of the house, not do them any real harm.

Relieved that there was evidence to support their claims, the Platts asked us how they might take their house back from the spirit. We recommended the services of a respected, local sensitive, who could help them make contact with the entity and negotiate an acceptable resolution.

Two weeks later, the sensitive came to their home and established a dialogue with the spirit. Shortly thereafter, the Platts' problems stopped. To this day, the house appears to be cleansed of paranormal activity.

When we researched the subject of white cats, we learned that they, too, have come to be associated with luck, both the good kind and the bad kind. As for why a human spirit chose to take the form of a white cat that autumn night in Norfolk, Virginia . . . your guess is as good as ours.

GHOST HUNTER'S MANUAL: THE SCIENTIFIC APPROACH

The scientific method has been around for a thousand years, maybe more, depending on how you define it. It's been used to prove the existence of bacteria, DNA, and black holes in the fabric of space. So why not supernatural phenomena?

If the public at large is ever going to understand the

spirit realm and its relationship to the world we know, it's going to require proof of that realm's existence. And why shouldn't it? We're a civilization of skeptics. Before we accept something, we want to be certain that it's real.

The first step in obtaining that proof is making observations. These may come in the form of personal experiences, but we can't verify personal experiences. So wherever possible, we try to capture our observations in video recordings, audio recordings, and digital meter readings of temperature changes and electromagnetic energy levels. In addition, we make extensive notes about when and where the data was collected, and under what circumstances.

Once we have this information, we come up with hypotheses. For example, we may say that spirits prefer to draw on a certain kind of energy when they're trying to manifest. The next step in the process is to test that hypothesis.

We can't do that in a laboratory, the way a research scientist would do it. Ghosts tend to appear in the places where people live and work, such as houses and hotels and theaters, which seldom offer the paranormal investigator the luxury of controlled conditions. So we do the best we can.

With the help of other investigators who we know we can trust, we try to duplicate as closely as possible the conditions under which we collected our first round of data. If we get the same results, we know that we're on to something. If we don't, we're back to square one.

But even if the results are the same, we still have a lot of work to do. Because we're not operating in a lab, we have to observe the phenomenon in different types of settings and under different conditions. And we have to capture the kind of data that will allow other observers to draw the same conclusions we did.

If it sounds like a lot of work, it is. But how else are we going to prove that ghosts and other supernatural entities exist in our world? Or that death isn't the barrier many of us believe it is?

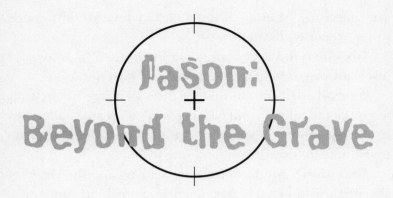

Jason:
Beyond the Grave

1995

In the depths of a long, gray winter, we got a call from a man named Erich Kohl. Erich, who was fifty-five years old, had lost his wife, Sonya, a little more than a year earlier. The two had been very close, very much in love all the way until the end.

Even over the phone, we could tell from the thickness in Erich's voice that talking about his wife still made him emotional. He said he had heard voices and seen odd sights in his house in the last year or so. He very much wanted us to come out to his house and conduct an investigation.

We picked a night that was mutually convenient. Then we packed up our van and visited Erich at his home. As we always do, we first sat down with the client and asked him about his experiences, so we could plan our investigation accordingly. However, Erich didn't seem eager to answer our questions. At one point, he said that we wouldn't need to set up any equipment.

"My wife is still here with me in the house," he told us. "I just want you to help me make contact with her."

We explained to him that we didn't engage in attempts to contact the dead. "But," I suggested as an alternative, "by carrying out an investigation, we may be able to confirm that your wife's spirit is still among us."

That wasn't good enough, he told us angrily. He *knew* she was still there. He just needed us to help him speak with her. If we couldn't do that, there was no reason for us to stay.

It's rare that a client asks us to vacate the premises, especially when we walked through the door only a few moments earlier. However, it was his house. We got back in the van, turned around, and went home.

A few weeks later, we got another call from Erich. He apologized for what he had said and asked us to conduct an investigation after all, without any attempts to communicate with the dead. At that point, he told us, he would be content simply knowing for certain that his wife's spirit was still present.

Honestly, we were still stinging a little from being kicked out of his house the first time. However, we weren't going to let that get in the way of the mission we had undertaken. The man was asking for help, and we weren't going to judge him—or turn him down.

Once again, we packed up the van. Once again, we made the trip to Erich's place. This time, he was a lot more hospitable. He apologized again, thanked us for coming, and said he would do whatever he could to accommodate us.

Grant and I investigated the house for three days straight. Unfortunately, we didn't find a single indication that it was haunted. No personal experiences, no video data, nothing at all. We knew Erich would be disappointed, but we had to give him the news.

As we had expected, he had a hard time accepting our conclusion. "She's here," he insisted quietly. "I'm sure of it."

"That may be," I conceded. "All I can tell you is that we couldn't document any evidence of her presence."

A few weeks later, I was again going over the audiotapes we had recorded in Erich's house, still trying to find something positive to tell him, when I caught what sounded like an EVP. It was faint and difficult to understand, but after running the tape back and forth several times, I thought I heard the name "Elena."

When I played it for Grant, he agreed. "We need to play it for Erich," he said, "but we can't tell him what we think it says."

That's the procedure we followed and follow still to this day. If you're going to verify a piece of evidence, you can't plant suggestions in someone's head. That person has to approach the data the same way you did, with an open mind.

The next day, we went back to Erich's house and told him that we wanted him to listen to a piece of tape. "Of course," he said. And he sat down next to the recorder, his eyes closed so he could concentrate better.

As soon as we reached that point in the tape, he broke down in tears. His shoulders heaved with emotion. Grant and I stood there silently, giving him his space, but we were eager to know what had happened.

Suddenly, he announced, "She's here! My wife is here in the house!" He looked and sounded as if he had won a great battle, even though his eyes were red from crying.

"How do you know?" I asked.

"She said, 'Elena,'" he told me, his voice thick with a mixture of joy and grief. "Who else but my wife would know the name of our stillborn daughter?"

It gave me chills to hear that.

"We had a secret," said Erich, "Sonya and I. We told people that we hadn't given the baby a name. But we called her Elena."

Apparently, they had made a promise to each other—that when one of them passed on, he or she would be on the other side with their daughter, waiting for the other one. After all, Elena was the only child Erich and his wife ever had.

GHOST HUNTER'S MANUAL: ELECTRONIC VOICE PHENOMENA

Back in 1959, a Swedish painter, performer, and film producer named Friedrich Jürgenson went out into the woods to record bird songs—one of his hobbies, apparently. Afterward, when he played his tape back, he heard something in addition to the bird sounds, something he didn't expect—human voices, even though he was the only person close enough to the tape recorder to be heard.

Curious, Jürgenson experimented further with his tape

recorder, taking it to even quieter places—both indoors and outdoors. His experiments were rewarded with additional voices, some of them uttering just a word and some uttering entire phrases. To his surprise, he recognized one of the voices as that of his dead mother, using phrases familiar to him to communicate from beyond the grave.

Because of this experience, Jürgenson concluded that the voices he had recorded were those of the dead. Was he correct in his assumption? Even today, paranormal investigators don't know for sure.

What we do know is that human-sounding voices have been recorded on tape recorders, digital voice recorders, video recorders, and other such devices a great many times since Jürgenson first heard those audio artifacts among his bird songs. Interestingly enough, these artifacts aren't audible at the time they're being recorded. It's only later on, when the recording is played back, that ghost hunters are able to take note of them.

We call them electronic voice phenomena, or EVPs. At T.A.P.S., we consider them one of the most valuable tools we have in our investigation of the paranormal.

Of course, there are skeptics who say that the voices detected by ghost hunters are simply the remnants of earlier recordings on our tapes. For a while, EVP researchers addressed this contention by using new, sealed tapes. Now, with the advent of digital recordings, the argument is irrelevant.

Skeptics also point to stray radio broadcasts as a possible source of EVPs. But as people who've had any experience with EVPs will tell you in a heartbeat, that argument is absurd. After all, these voices are responding to questions, commenting on specific situations, and sometimes even addressing the researcher by name. The chances of a stray radio broadcast accomplishing this are pretty remote.

What's more, the voices captured aren't the voices of professional broadcasters. They're often the voices of children, or the elderly, or people with heavy accents. They may be full of emotion. They may mispronounce words, or swear, or mumble, or do any number of things professional broadcasters would avoid.

So whose voices are they? Are they the dead trying to communicate with us? Most EVP researchers believe they are, and the types of things we hear in EVPs would seem to back up that contention.

Sometimes the voice we record is asking for help. Sometimes it is demanding that people leave a certain place. Sometimes it seems to be telling someone that it misses that person's company.

Clearly, these are the kinds of things we would hear if we could communicate with the dead. On occasion, our clients will even recognize the voice in question. They'll tell us that it belongs to a friend or relative who has passed over.

For instance, in one of our televised cases, a man named Adam Zubroski called us in to investigate some bizarre occurrences in his house. We recorded a number of EVPs there, but we couldn't make out the words. When we played them back for Adam, he recognized the voice as that of his grandfather. The reason we couldn't understand him was that he was speaking in Polish.

How do you create the best conditions for recording an EVP? First off, avoid the use of cheap recorders. Do your best to find something better. Even a portable stereo has better recording capabilities than something the size and quality of a Walkman.

Second, use an external microphone. Any recording device, no matter how sophisticated it is, will give off some kind of internal sound. If you're depending on a built-in microphone, this sound will drown out an EVP, making it very difficult to understand—if you can hear it at all.

Third, don't economize when it comes to the quality of your disks or tapes. Remember, these are what hold your valuable recordings. Spend the extra couple of bucks on quality and assure yourself of better sound.

Fourth, turn on a little background noise. You may want to try running water, TV or radio static (also known as white noise), or even a vacuum cleaner. The idea is to create a steady but meaningless stream of sound.

After all, spirits require a great deal of energy to make noises that will register on our recordings. This is why ghost hunters often hear only mumbles and groans when they review their data—because the spirits they're contacting don't have the energy they need to produce recognizable words or phrases.

If you supply them with background noise, they can piece together sounds from the static to more easily form words. Not enough, maybe, for us to hear them with our ears alone. However, our recorders are more sensitive than the human auditory apparatus, so we're making it easier for the spirits to be heard.

On the other hand, you don't want to run the risk of overpowering the recording, so make certain to unplug anything in the room that you don't need to create background noise or record your EVP. Remember, almost any machine that uses electricity will make some kind of sound. When you play back your data later on, that sound may fool you into thinking it's been made by a ghost.

The next step is to establish some comparative noises on your recording. Comparative noises are coughs, heavy breathing, footsteps, banging on walls, words and phrases spoken in surrounding rooms at various volumes and pitches, and so on—any sound that could possibly be mistaken for an EVP later on. When you're done, announce on your disk or tape that you've completed the comparative noise part of the program and you're ready to record in earnest.

At this point, just set down your recorder and relax. Get comfortable. Take a breath, clear your mind, and sit still. Some people like to say a prayer, but that's really an individual choice.

A number of ghost hunters believe asking questions of a spirit helps the odds of recording an EVP. If you choose to do this, be sure to keep your questions simple and straightforward. For starters, try, "What's your name?" Steer clear of questions like, "How often did you think about going to your mother's house, and if it *was* often, which days did you decide not to do it?"

Don't forget to leave a long pause between questions so the spirit has time to answer. Give it about three times as long as you would give a living person. And don't whisper. When you pose your questions, speak loudly and clearly.

Whatever you do, don't speak directly into the microphone. After all, when you play back the tape you'll have the volume cranked up so you can hear every little sound.

If you come booming over the speaker at fifty thousand decibels, your chances of hearing anything ever again are slim to none.

When you're done with your recording, you may politely thank the spirit. Of course, you don't *have* to do this. Like praying beforehand, it's a matter of personal choice. In any case, respect the spirit you're trying to contact. If you can help it once you've heard what it has to say, make every effort to do so.

Don't start off by asking spirits if they know they're dead. Would *you* want to hear that? Also, try to keep in mind the time period in which they lived. Spirits who died back in the 1600s won't have any idea what a "recorder" or a "camera" is, so if you mention such items you'll only confuse them.

Always keep in mind the reason for your recording— so that you can document the presence of a supernatural entity on the premises. For your data to be scientifically sound, it has to be as clear and irrefutable as possible. If someone can say your EVP was something else, it's of considerably less value to you.

As with any evidence, you have to put an EVP to the test before you can rely on it. If you think you've got an EVP, ask someone else to listen to it. If that person comes to the same conclusion you did, you're a step closer to confirmation. If a third person hears the same thing . . . maybe then you can call it evidence of a haunting.

Jason: The Atheists

1996

Not everyone believes in God. But as we've learned over the years, atheism isn't necessarily a protection from the supernatural.

Lawrence and Thea Bodine, a couple in Pawtucket, Rhode Island, had no affiliation with organized religion. They had raised their only child, a fourteen-year-old boy named Sam, to treat other people as he would want to be treated—essentially, to obey the golden rule. But for the Bodines, God wasn't part of the plan.

Grant and I, along with Ed Gaines and Brittney Selden, arrived at the Bodine house at about four in the afternoon. It was a hot day in mid-August of 1996, one of those clear days when the sky doesn't have a cloud in it. Lawrence and

Thea came out to greet us as soon as they saw us pull up into their driveway.

We could see that they had been under a lot of stress lately. But then, they were scared of what might be inhabiting their home. Until recently, they had been as skeptical of the paranormal as they were of religion, but what they had been through lately appeared to have changed their minds.

They had seen faces reflected in windows, and also in other surfaces. However, when they turned to find the source of the reflection, there wasn't anyone there. Even when they were alone, they could feel someone touch their arms and legs, and sometimes even grab them.

Lawrence and Thea had woken at night to see what appeared to be a human figure standing at the foot of their bed. As far as they could tell, it wasn't anyone they knew. On other occasions, they felt something tugging at their bedspread and woke to find that it had been yanked clear off the bed.

While Ed and I interviewed Lawrence and Thea, Grant and Brittney conducted a walkthrough of the house. It was small but tidy, with two bedrooms on the second floor. The first floor contained a third bedroom, a living room, a kitchen, and a bathroom. Unsurprisingly, in light of what the Bodines had told us over the phone, the place was devoid of religious symbols of any kind.

Our investigation that night didn't turn up any hard evidence, but we had enough personal experiences to conclude that the Bodine home was full of paranormal activity. We were touched by things we couldn't see. We caught glimpses of faces in reflective surfaces, just as the Bodines had.

To our minds, the incidents in the house had been caused by a human spirit. After all, its behavior took several different forms, occurred in several different parts of the house, and was ultimately harmless to the living.

We believed it was just looking for attention. However, we didn't know for what purpose, so we suggested to the Bodines that we invite a sensitive to participate in their case. His job would be to make contact with the spirit, find out why it was in the house, and try to get it to leave. The family agreed to this strategy, and we brought in a sensitive we had worked with before.

He was indeed able to make contact with the spirit, a man who had lived in the house previously and had perished some years earlier. However, the spirit had been unaware of its passing. As far as it knew, it was still alive. It saw people sleeping in the bedroom where it used to sleep, wondered who they were, and attempted to wake them in order to find out.

The sensitive explained to the spirit that its mortal form was deceased, and that it needed to pass on. The spirit was understandably upset by the news, but eventually came to accept it. No longer confused, it departed our world for the next one.

We left the Bodines with a lot of questions, not just about the paranormal but about spirituality in general. We don't know if they ever found any satisfactory answers. However, we do know that they haven't seen any spirits in the more than twelve years since our visit.

GHOST HUNTER'S MANUAL: HUMAN HAUNTINGS

In a human haunting, the entity or entities involved are aware of their surroundings. This means that they are also aware of the living beings around them—in other words, you and me. This puts them in an entirely different class from the figures we perceive in the context of a residual haunting (a paranormal phenomenon that repeats itself mindlessly, like a broken record).

Remember to treat these spirits like living human beings. Though people are generally good, they have a wide array of personalities—and so do human entities. They need to be talked to as humans, with respect. After all, they once had families, jobs, ambitions, and so on.

While residual hauntings have no intent behind them, human spirits always have a purpose in mind. Mainly, they want to get attention. What's more, they can tell when they're getting it and when they're not, so they're more likely to pull off the kind of stunts that get them noticed.

Sometimes their attention-getting maneuvers include moving objects. Because this kind of effort requires energy, human entities are generally limited in what they can accomplish. Most of the time, they can move only very light objects. However, they have been known to push around objects up to ten pounds in weight.

Most of the time you will find that these spirits are not confined to one particular area. On the contrary, they can move around freely, often more so than you and I. And wherever they are, they will acknowledge the existence of human beings and even try to communicate with them directly.

This is why most people fear human spirits—because they like direct contact, and that kind of contact can be a discomfiting and even alarming experience. But these entities, while mischievous at times, aren't trying to hurt anyone. In fact, they may even be benevolent, depending on the reason they're remaining with us.

One thing is always true of human spirits: They want to remain exactly where they are. Homeowners, on the other hand, usually want these spirits out of their lives, and understandably so. Unfortunately, it's not exactly a piece of cake to get rid of them. They aren't inhuman entities (which we'll get to later on), so religious provocation isn't an effective course of action. Like the spirits themselves, the people haunted by them are limited in what they can do.

The only way we have found to rid a home of a human entity is to somehow make contact with it—a sensitive can be a big help in this regard—and convince it to cross over to the other side. The key here is to remember that the entity is lingering in our world for a reason. It may be that he's worried about a living person he left behind, or that he's attached to a possession he had when he was alive, or that there was some work he never got the opportunity to complete.

Maybe he's haunting the house he used to live in and wants its current occupants to leave. Or it could be he's looking for someone important to him, who may be just as dead as he is. Or he just can't accept the fact that he died, and remains with us strictly out of stubbornness.

We have seen cases where a child is able to see or hear the entity, and this encourages the entity to stick around. On other occasions, we have come to the conclusion that someone in the house is sensitive to paranormal phenomena and is giving off an energy that the entity finds appealing. We have even worked cases in which the entity is remaining behind because he fears judgment on the other side.

Whatever the reason, it needs to be addressed. The lingering spirit must be relieved of the concerns that are keeping him in the world of the living. He must be gently but firmly separated from the people, places, or possessions to which he has become attached. Then, and only then, will he go on to his eternal rest and allow the homeowner to get some rest of his own.

Grant:
Allie

1997

This case is one we don't often talk about because it involved a relative of one of our investigators. The investigator's family believed that his sister Allie, who was fourteen, was becoming schizophrenic.

For one thing, she was hearing voices, the kind that made her feel worthless with their taunts. For another, she was experiencing wild mood swings. And little by little, it was getting worse.

Of course, we wished we could help Allie. But we're not doctors. There didn't seem to be anything we could do.

Then, one day, as Jason and I were discussing her situation, we came up with the theory that Allie wasn't schizophrenic at all. What if she was just becoming sensitive to paranormal phenomena? What if she was hearing spirit voices and taking on their emotions as if they were her own?

Of course, as the spirits discovered that she could hear them, they would naturally flock to her like moths to a flame. This, in turn, would increase the severity of her situation. Anyway, that was our theory. We asked Allie and her family if they would give us a chance to put it to the test.

Our investigator advised his parents to give us permission. On his say-so, they agreed. Allie was up for it as well. Soon afterward, we spent some time with her, waiting for her to have one of her supposedly schizophrenic experiences.

It didn't take long before she had an attack, as she called it, of voices talking "close to her head." We ran an audio recorder beside her, hoping to obtain some evidence of paranormal activity. We also had her write down what was being said to her as best she could make it out.

When we researched the name and information she had spat out during her attack, we found that it had a basis in local history. And later, as we reviewed the audio data we had collected, we caught a number of EVPs. The words we heard in them matched exactly what Allie had written down for us.

In our view, this was enough evidence to support the contention that she wasn't schizophrenic. She was just becoming sensitive to the paranormal. At that point, we focused our efforts on counseling her and making sure that she could gain control of her newfound abilities. In time, she was able to manage both the mood swings and the voices, keeping them from overwhelming her.

Allie's case was just one of many in which someone is diagnosed with schizophrenia when, in fact, he or she is simply becoming sensitive to paranormal phenomena. I should know. There was a time when I saw and heard things other people didn't and was ready to pronounce myself a schizophrenic.

Science always tries to label everything, and it has done a hell of a job. But sometimes the label it puts on something is inaccurate. Sometimes the answer falls outside the realm of established scientific knowledge.

Unfortunately, it's difficult to distinguish between schizophrenia and a mere increase in sensitivity. After all, the "symptoms" are almost exactly the same. The subject experiences a high level of anxiety, speaks in disconnected and confusing ways, falls prey to poor reasoning and judgment, has memory lapses, is afflicted with eating and sleeping difficulties, sees and hears things no one else can see or hear, and withdraws from the company of others.

Schizophrenia typically shows up in a person's late teens or early twenties. It's often the same with sensitivity. Just before those years the body is going through a significant transformation, so we probably shouldn't be surprised that these conditions show up when they do.

While we're on the subject, we should dispel some of the myths about schizophrenia. For instance, those afflicted with it do not have a "split personality," as many people believe, and they are not prone to violence. Schizophrenia is simply a disorder in which certain thought patterns and processes are disrupted, causing a disconnect between the schizophrenic and what we recognize as reality.

This is not an illness caused by bad parenting, so there's no point in tossing around blame. It doesn't reflect a weakness in character on the part of the person afflicted. All it reflects is a biochemical disturbance in the brain.

Schizophrenia affects approximately one person in a hundred, and it has no preference for men or women. Apparently, about a third of those who experience a schizophrenic episode will never experience another one in their lifetimes. Another third will have episodes from time to time, but will exhibit no symptoms in between. It's only the last third that requires continuing medical treatment, which has improved in leaps and bounds over the years.

I understand that we have people out there who are truly mentally ill. It would be naïve of me to say otherwise, and people who are concerned that they might be ill shouldn't hesitate to seek medical attention. But we need to be careful about the labels we place on people, because maybe—just maybe—a person we think is schizophrenic has developed a talent rather than an illness.

Grant: The Haunted Trailer Park

1997

This case took place in the month of June, in a trailer park in central Vermont that abutted more than 150 acres of lush, green forest land. It was as cool and quiet there as you please, even in the heat of summer, with the fragrance of pine trees filling your nostrils everywhere you went. A real nice place.

And if you believed the residents, thoroughly haunted.

The lady who contacted us for help had a double-wide, which—as you can tell from the name—is twice the size of a regular trailer. She had four bedrooms, a little manicured front lawn, and a bit of an ego. "The people who live here," she said, "are your typical trailer people," implying that she wasn't.

Her opinion of herself didn't seem to matter to whomever or whatever was plaguing the trailer park. She had her problems just like everybody else. The kind of problems, apparently, that made her skin crawl.

One night, she had been watching her TV when the screen was suddenly claimed by static. She turned it off and back on again, hoping to get rid of it, but it didn't go away. Then, before her eyes, a human-looking face took shape.

As time went on, it happened again. And again. First the static, then the face emerging from it. The lady didn't recognize the face, but she couldn't avoid the frightening feeling that it was full of evil intent.

Some of the other residents had had experiences as well. One woman told us that someone had stolen knives from her silverware drawer, even though her trailer was always locked when she wasn't around. A man told us that his television had started turning on and off on its own. Objects were moving around people's trailers. Threatening voices were coming through stereo systems that had been turned off, and in some cases weren't even plugged into electrical sockets.

Two cats and a dog had gone missing in the past few weeks. Only one—the cat belonging to the lady in the double-wide—had managed to find its way back. But it had done so without its tail.

Because there were so many complaints, and in so many homes, we wound up making more than one visit to the trailer park. Each time we brought a full complement of video and audio equipment, electromagnetic field meters, and digital thermometers. And each time, we investigated a different trailer.

Unfortunately, we didn't find anything worth talking about. One of the residents had a bizarre noise coming from her radio, but that was about it. On the other hand, the place was right in the middle of the woods, so Jason and I decided to search the outlying areas as well.

On the last night of our investigation, which was Saturday, we decided to survey the woods north of the trailer park and see if we could find anything there. We took a video camera with us in case we found anything we thought might be evidence. But for a while, it looked as if we were wasting our time.

All we saw were trees, rocks, bushes . . . the usual things you find in a forest. There was a little breeze, so every now and then a branch would sway a little, but that was about it. And the only sounds we heard were birdsongs, which became fewer and farther between as twilight gave way to full darkness.

Then Jay noticed something—a cage sitting there in the middle of the woods, the kind that is used to catch possums or raccoons. Then I saw a pile of rocks nearby, and I knew we had hit on something. As we got closer, we recognized the pile of rocks—which had a big, smooth, flat one on the top—as a makeshift altar.

The top stone had dark stains on it, the kind that are made by blood. I was hunkered down on my haunches, inspecting the altar more closely, when Jay called me over to the cage. He wanted me to take a look at something.

"What is it?" I asked.

He pointed. There was something inside the cage. A tail. The kind you might find on a house cat.

Jay made a sound of disgust. "Nice."

Before long, we came across another clue—a circle made of small stones, with a pentagram cut into the earth inside it. Both of us had seen this type of thing before, though it was never a welcome sight.

"A summoning circle," I breathed.

Jay nodded.

Summoning circles are used to bring demonic entities into our world. Sometimes they're built on natural gateways like bent-over trees or rock formations, but others are created from scratch. This one was of the latter variety.

We had stumbled onto a cult of devil-worshipers. No question about it. The cage with the tail in it, the altar, the circle—it was the only possible explanation.

Now we knew what was happening to the people in the trailer park. Someone was conducting demonic rituals in the woods, bringing inhuman entities to the area that manifested in the form of voices, television images, and moving shadows. As long as the rituals continued, the supernatural presences would remain—and maybe even become more dangerous as time went on.

We could have returned to the trailer park at that point. We already knew what we had ventured out into the woods to find out. But we kept going, wondering what else there was to discover.

That's the ghost hunter in us. We don't like to stop until we've gathered all the evidence it's possible to gather. And since there's no way to know when that will be, we just go on for as long as we can.

Finally, our perseverance was rewarded. In the distance, among the trees, there was a flicker of yellow light. It looked like a campfire. *Maybe just some kids,* I thought. But I didn't believe it.

Judging from his expression, Jay didn't believe it either.

I pointed in the direction of the firelight and he nodded. Careful not to make any noise, we got closer. And closer still. Finally, we stopped and concealed ourselves behind some trees.

We were far enough away to avoid being seen, but close enough to record what we had encountered. Using my camera's zoom feature, I was able to make out some of the details of the ceremony. I could see half a dozen men, gathered around an altar like the one we had seen earlier. They were chanting and saying things I couldn't make out, though I could pretty much guess the essence of it.

Suddenly, I heard something come up behind us. As I turned, I was sure I was going to find myself face to face with a large animal. But there was nothing there.

Jay must have heard the same thing, because he had whirled as well. He shook his head and muttered something beneath his breath. Then he turned back to the ceremony, and so did I.

For the next five minutes or so, I got the details of the ritual on tape. Then I felt it again—the presence of something big and beastlike behind me. But when I reacted, I saw again that the woods were empty in that direction. No large animal, nothing at all. And yet, I had been so certain.

As before, Jay had felt the same thing. And as before, he didn't look happy about it. Turning back to the ceremony, I resumed my videotaping.

But after a while, I noticed something strange. One of the demon-worshipers was looking at me. Not just in my general direction, but straight *at* me. It gave me a chill. And then Jay whispered something to me.

"The light on the camera," he said. "Cover it."

Of course, I thought—the infrared light on the video camera. It was just a tiny red dot, but it was still a light. And all around us there was nothing but darkness, so it was easy for the demon-worshipper to pick us out.

I slowly covered the light with my hand and whispered to Jay, "We've gotta go."

We started backing away, trying not to make too much noise. But before we got very far, we realized there were people behind us—a number of them, how many exactly we weren't sure. Four or five, maybe.

Jay and I could have run, but we held our ground. After all, they knew these woods better than we did. If we ran, they would certainly catch us, and we were outnumbered. On the other hand, if we stayed where we were, we could make it seem as if we weren't much of a threat.

Quickly, I popped out the tape and gave it to Jay to hide in one of his pockets. Then I popped in a blank tape and hoped the occultists hadn't seen the exchange as they approached.

A moment later, we were surrounded. One of the demon-worshippers, a guy with a thin face and a beard, asked us our names. The last thing we wanted was for these guys to track us down and harm our families, so we gave them fake names.

They didn't ask for proof. The bearded guy just held his hand out and asked for the videotape. I hesitated because I didn't want to make it seem like I was giving in too easily.

The bearded guy said, "You can hand it to me or we can take it from you. In fact, I'm hoping I have to take it." He looked like he meant it.

With feigned reluctance, I opened the camera again

and popped out the blank tape. Then I handed it over. The bearded guy gave the tape to one of his companions and said, "Now the other one."

Obviously, he had seen me hand the tape to my partner. Jay and I looked at each other. We were both ready to fight to keep the tape, if that was what it took. Then we heard more footfalls in the dark around us, signifying the approach of additional adversaries. The odds against us were getting worse. Frowning, Jay reached into his pocket and turned over the tape with all the footage on it. I felt my heart sink. It would have been amazing to have a visual record of a genuine occult ceremony, but I had to agree with my partner that it wasn't worth our lives.

Still, they talked about punishing us for what we had seen. We didn't tell them that we were paranormal investigators, or that we were trying to help the people in the trailer park. We said we had heard that there was something going on in the woods, and wanted to see what it was—nothing more than that.

They still looked like they wanted to beat the hell out of us or worse, so Jay mentioned that we had sent a buddy of ours back to town so the police would know where we were in case something happened to us. It was a lie, of course.

But it made them hesitate. Then the bearded guy got right up in our faces and told us it was in our best interest not to talk about what we had seen there. We assured him that we wouldn't—a promise we had no intention of keeping.

"Then get out of here," said the bearded man.

He didn't have to say it twice. We turned and walked back through the woods to the trailer park. But every time we heard the slightest noise behind us, we were sure the occultists had seen through our lie and changed their minds.

A few weeks later, we went back to the same spot with fresh videotape, hoping to catch the occultists in the act again. This time, we brought a few friends. After all, we didn't just want to capture new footage—we wanted to get our tape back.

Unfortunately, everything was gone—the cages, the altars, even the summoning circles. There was no evidence that the occultists had ever existed.

On the other hand, occult activity in the park appeared to die down over the next few months, and finally came to a stop. I wish I could tell you what happened to the group we ran into. More than likely, they found another secluded place in which to carry on their demon-worship.

The important thing was that the people in the trailer park were free from the inhuman spirits that had haunted them.

GHOST HUNTER'S MANUAL: THE INFRARED CAMERA

Why use an infrared camera in the course of our ghost-hunting activities? The answer is simple. An IR camera picks up wavelengths of electromagnetic radiation that our eyes aren't equipped to pick up on their own.

What seems to us like total darkness as we enter a room looking for evidence of spirits is often not total darkness at all. It's just that the available radiation is at the part of the light spectrum that we can't pick up. We can see red, which is the color with the longest wavelength that registers with us. However, we can't see infrared, which has an even longer wavelength—somewhere between 750 nanometers and one micrometer.

If you're wondering what even longer wavelengths of electromagnetic radiation are called, check out the little oven on your kitchen counter. When you heat up your leftovers from the night before, you're using microwaves, which have a wavelength a bit longer than that of infrared radiation. On the other end of the spectrum, violet is the color with the shortest visible wavelength. Below that is ultraviolet, which—like infrared—is invisible to the naked eye.

As with every piece of ghost-hunting equipment, there are certain drawbacks to the use of an IR camera. For one thing, it won't allow you to see or record in color, because you're operating beyond the boundaries of the visible spectrum. For another, every shade in the image will be reversed. In other words, black will look white and objects that are darker in color will appear lighter.

However, it also has a number of advantages. For instance, it enables us to navigate under conditions that would otherwise keep us—literally—in the dark. But the main reason we use IR cameras is to see things we wouldn't see even in broad daylight. That is, evidence of paranormal phenomena.

Investigators operate under the theory that spirits, like people, give off a certain amount of thermal energy. Heat energy is detectable in the infrared band. So if there's a spirit around, an IR camera may be in a position to capture it.

Of course, that's assuming you're pointing it in the right direction. As always, a camera is only as good as the person operating it. If you know what you're doing and where to search for paranormal activity, your chances of success in finding it will always be that much greater.

One last point. The IR monitor, which is set up at a central location in the investigation, always seems to attract a lot of attention. Sometimes a number of team members will crowd around the monitor and just watch the screen, forgetting that there are other aspects of the investigation to keep an eye on.

It's an interesting and sometimes even amusing phenomenon, and it's not hard to explain. After all, we've been watching television all our lives. Gazing at the IR screen is a lot like watching TV, and it has the added appeal of being a live feed. Besides, as much as we may say we like to work independently, humans are social animals. If there's a place to congregate, we'll find it.

But investigators have to remember that they've got other responsibilities in an investigation. They have to spread their time and energy. One good idea is to hook up the infrared monitor to a VCR, so the images taken by the IR camera can be recorded and viewed later on.

If the lead investigator feels it's important to have someone watching the monitor, make it just one member of the team, or two at most. And let them know you want them to limit their conversations. Talk can be distracting in an investigation, and whoever's watching a monitor really needs to concentrate on what he's doing.

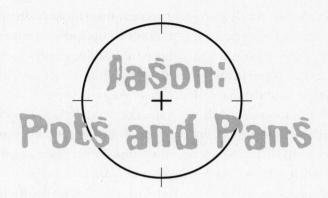

Jason:
Pots and Pans

1997

Tim Cunningham wasn't a neat freak or anything like that. It was just that by the summer of 1997 he had been living alone for a while, and was used to everything being in its place. The last thing he wanted—or expected—was to come home and find his pots and pans stacked on the kitchen floor.

At first, Tim thought someone was pulling a prank on him—someone with access to the brand-new three-floor condominium he had settled into just a few weeks earlier. Then it occurred to him that he hadn't known anyone in the development long enough to trust them with his key. The more he considered the stack of pots and pans, the more uncomfortable he felt.

He could have understood if a burglar had broken in and taken money or something of value. But there was no sign of a break-in, no door locks broken, no windows smashed. And when he checked his valuables in his bedroom drawer, he saw they were still right where he left them.

So what was going on?

Tim was about to call the police when he got the feeling someone was watching him. Darting a glance over his shoulder in the direction of the living room, he was relieved to find no one there. But something else caught his eye.

Not a person, but the state of the living room itself. Walking into the center of it, Tim was shocked to see that the furniture had been rearranged. His couch, which had been on one side of the room, was now on the other. His easy chair was facing the wall instead of the television. The television was sitting on the floor under the window, and the ottoman was on its side, nowhere near the easy chair.

The coffee table was upside down. The standing lamp that had belonged to Tim's parents was unplugged and in the wrong corner of the room. And the wall hangings were all mixed up, one of them even turned upside down.

It was getting stranger and stranger. And the more Tim thought about it, the more he had to wonder what the police would say. More than likely, they would think he was crazy. Whoever heard of an intruder who emptied your kitchen cupboards and rearranged your living room?

Maybe I *am* crazy, Tim thought. Maybe I did all this stuff myself, and I'm losing my mind. It made about as much sense as anything else.

That was when he caught a glimpse of something through his living room window—something small and dark against the gathering twilight, scurrying away from

Tim's property and finally vanishing into the woods at the edge of the development. It wasn't running on all fours, so it wasn't an animal. So what could it be?

And did it have anything to do with what had happened in his condo? Tim sat down heavily on his couch, lit a cigarette to calm himself, and tried to figure out what to do. If he couldn't call the police, who *could* he call?

In the end, he contacted T.A.P.S.

By the time Grant and I arrived in Charleston, Rhode Island, with our team of investigators, Tim had put away his cookware, only to have it removed from his cupboards again almost every day. He had restored his living room furniture to its original configuration and seen it rearranged more times than he cared to count. His electricity had cut out on a regular basis, certain items had gone missing only to turn up in places where he had already looked for them, and he constantly got the feeling that he was being watched.

The small, black thing he had seen scurrying across the grass? Tim had seen it on other occasions as well, or maybe there were a whole bunch of them. He was too agitated to even speculate.

Grant and I sat down and spoke with Tim in his living room while our associates worked around us, setting up a video camera and various other pieces of equipment. We noted that the furniture in the room looked fine to us. Tim told us that he had just put everything back in its place a few hours before we arrived.

We went outside with Tim to investigate the place where he had first spotted the small, black thing. There was no sign of anything unusual there, but it was still daylight, and paranormal activity seldom takes place until after dark.

We noted that the condo development was surrounded by dense forest. Apparently, other such developments were scheduled to be built in the area, but none of them had broken ground yet. As a result, the place had a lonely feel to it, as if the trees were pressing in on it.

Returning to Tim's condo, we asked to see his kitchen. He said we probably wouldn't notice anything amiss, as he had put all his stuff away just that morning. But when we entered the kitchen, we saw a pile of pots and pans in the middle of the floor.

"This is what it's like," he told us, a note of resignation in his voice.

Grant and I gave him a hand putting away his cookware. When we were done, we decided to move the camera and an audio recorder that we had placed in the living room into the kitchen. After taking care of that, we asked Tim to show us the rest of his condo, including his bedroom, his computer room, and his basement.

Everything looked to be in order upstairs. As we went down into the basement, our team moved down there with us to set up a camera and other recording equipment. After all, Tim had complained about the electricity cutting out. We wanted to keep an eye on the fuse box to see if anyone was tampering with it.

While Grant and I checked out the basement's nooks and crannies, Tim took out his lighter and lit a cigarette. If he wasn't a chain-smoker, he was pretty close. I made a mental note of the fact. You never know what's going to become a significant piece of information in an investigation.

When we came up from the basement, we expected to be able to sit down with Tim and round out our knowledge of his experiences. What we found was that the living room furniture had been rearranged. The couch had been moved across the room, the pictures in the walls were in different places, and certain other pieces were turned on their sides or upside down.

The whole time we were in the basement, we hadn't heard a sound to indicate that furniture was being moved on the floor above us. Our audio recorder hadn't picked up anything either. Tim just looked at us and shrugged. Grant and I checked to make sure that our people hadn't moved anything in the living room, for one reason or another. No one had.

Unfortunately, we hadn't caught anything with our cameras, because one was in the basement and the other had been moved into the kitchen. To remedy the situation, we relocated the camera that was in the basement to the living room. It would mean that we wouldn't be able to record anything that happened in the basement, but we could monitor that part of the house in person.

Then Tim made a suggestion. "I've got a video camera," he said. "Want to borrow it?" We accepted the offer, taking out the tape Tim had in there and putting in one of our own. Then we set it up in the basement.

We had just finished when Tim reported that his lighter, which he always kept in his right front pocket, was missing. He couldn't remember the last time he had used it, but I could. It was down in the basement, about twenty minutes earlier.

Soon afterward, Grant and I hunkered down in the basement, along with Tim and the other members of our team. For an hour or so, nothing happened. Then our

EMF meters spiked, indicating a rise in electromagnetic power levels in the space around us. A second later, the basement went black.

We still had our flashlights, so we could get around just fine. When we checked out the fuse box, we could see that one of the fuses had blown. As Tim replaced the fuse, we rewound the video data collected with our camera in the living room. As far as we could tell, nothing had changed when the electricity cut out.

Then we checked the video from the kitchen. What we saw there was astonishing—a two-to-three-foot-tall black figure rapidly stacking Tim's pots and pans in the middle of the floor. While our team remained in the basement, Grant and I bolted upstairs to confirm what we had seen on the tape.

Sure enough, we saw the cookware piled on the floor, pretty much as we had found it earlier that evening. We hadn't heard a sound but the cupboards were completely empty. And this time, there was another object sitting among the pots and pans. It was Tim's cigarette lighter.

When morning came, we packed up and returned to Rhode Island to review our data. We didn't end up finding anything else, but the video of the little, black figure tampering with the cookware in the kitchen was pretty solid evidence. Clearly, Tim had a supernatural problem on his hands.

Considering his development's location in the middle of the woods and the appearance of the intruder in his kitchen, it seemed to us that the entity giving him fits was an elemental—one that resented the intrusion of civilization in the area. We had had some prior experience with elementals, so we knew that they had to be treated differently than other entities.

If it were an inhuman entity, we would have tried to oust it from the house through religious provocation. If it were a human entity, we would have encouraged Tim to try to reason with it. But it wasn't either of those things.

As frustrating as it can be, the only way to deal with an elemental is to let it wear itself out. That was our advice to Tim. "Just don't react to it," I told him. "Let it do its thing. Eventually it will get tired of it and go somewhere else."

Tim gratefully did as we suggested. Last we heard, there has been substantially less activity in his home, though the elemental hadn't disappeared entirely. Unfortunately, it takes a little longer in some cases for such an entity to lose interest and leave the homeowner alone.

GHOST HUNTER'S MANUAL: THE EMF METER

The EMF (electromagnetic field) meter is one of the most powerful tools at the disposal of the paranormal investigator. However, in order to use this device effectively, he has to know what he's doing. To begin with, he has to understand the nature of electrical and magnetic fields.

Basically, these fields are the invisible lines of energy that emanate from any machine that uses electricity as its power source. Power lines produce electromagnetic fields as well, since they carry electricity from place to place.

When the voltage supplied to a man-made device increases, the strength of the resulting electrical fields increases as well. So does the strength of the magnetic fields, which are a byproduct of the flow of electricity along metal wires. Magnetic fields are measured in units called gausses.

The theory we subscribe to as paranormal investigators is that supernatural entities create changes in a room's magnetic fields. Sometimes they're subtle changes, nearly impossible to detect. At other times they're big, abrupt swings in energy levels that are almost impossible to miss.

On most EMF detectors, each LED light at the x10 setting represents 1.0 milligauss. What you're looking for is a reading between 2.0 and 7.0 miligausses. That's because power lines generate fields below that level, so anything above it is suspect. But even if you get a steady 7.0, it's no guarantee that you're looking at something supernatural. You still have to make certain your reading can't be explained by the presence of a man-made power source.

You may also see a reading that fluctuates for no discernible reason. Let's say you're standing in a room and your meter is reading 2.0, but then it suddenly jumps to 9.0, and then drops back to 2.0. If you can't find a reason for it, you may have evidence of a paranormal incident on your hands.

Or maybe you're registering normal background readings for a period of time, and then they drop. You look around and try to find an explanation for what happened. If you can't, it may be an indication that there's a spirit in the area sucking up energy because it's trying to manifest.

Of course, as with all of our equipment, we're using the EMF detectors to debunk claims of the paranormal rather than to prove them. When we find EMF spikes that we can't explain, they could be due to something paranormal, but what we are looking for are false-positives, or conditions that could cause the appearance of paranormal activity without there actually being any.

It's important to keep in mind that high EMFs can have adverse effects on people, especially people who are hyper-sensitive to such fields. What might seem like a reaction to the paranormal could be the result of prolonged exposure to EMFs—the kind generated by old wiring in the walls, grounded-out copper lines, or alarm clocks. Some common effects of EMF hyper-sensitivity are: nausea, paranoia, headaches, and skin irritations.

Because it's so easy to mistake a naturally occurring EMF for a supernatural one, you should always try to correlate your reading with some other observation. A cold spot, an orb recorded in a photograph, or even a strange feeling on the part of an investigator can lend credibility to an unusual EMF indication. That's why it's always a good idea for the person with the EMF detector to partner with someone—especially someone with a video camera. Then, when the EMF registers something interesting, the camera is right there to take a picture.

In any case, the incident should be documented, like anything that takes place in the course of an investigation. The person handling the EMF detector should write down the time as well as the location, so he can go back to the spot later on and see if he obtains the same results.

When an EMF detector is used to best advantage, it's a beautiful thing. But too often, the person using it is unfamiliar with its limitations. After all, this device was never intended to be employed in paranormal investigations. It was designed to measure the electromagnetic emissions generated by microwave ovens and high-tension electrical wires, not the spirits of the departed.

That's why EMF meters are sensitive to such man-made devices as washing machines, televisions, microwave ovens, and even clock radios. They also register live power lines. If your fellow investigator's video camera is too close to your EMF detector, it will probably react to that as well.

So it's not unusual to get an EM spike now and then. And of course, when that happens, you're tempted to believe you've identified paranormal activity. But before you get too excited, check your surroundings. Make sure there's no man-made device in the immediate area that could be responsible for your reading—say, a light going on, or a refrigerator entering a new cycle and pulling more juice.

You don't have to worry about this problem as much if you're using the Trifield Natural EMF Meter. Unlike other such meters, it ignores most man-made devices. Still, you need to be on your guard against jumping to conclusions. It's only after you've eliminated every possible power source, and you're still in the range of 2.0 to 7.0 miligausses, that you can say you've detected paranormal activity.

Too often, people forget that an EMF meter is a sensitive piece of equipment. If you jerk it this way and that, making sudden movements, you'll almost certainly get a false reading. What you want to do is gently slide it from side to side and then up and down, in a slow, steady pattern. Then, when you get a result worth recording, it'll be because of what you discovered and not because of how you handled the detector.

If you've got a new EMF detector, get accustomed to it before you take it on an investigation. Expose it to your television, your microwave, and so on, to see how it reacts to these electrical sources. Vary the distance from each source, so you get an idea of how sensitive it is at thirty feet, twenty feet, and ten feet.

There's just one other thing you need to do before you take your EMF meter along on an investigation, and that's to get hold of some extra batteries. Batteries drain more quickly than you might think, as we've learned from bitter experience, and you want to make sure you're ready for anything.

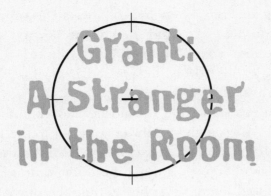

Grant: A Stranger in the Room

1997

Joe Tandy, an information technology executive with a major company in a Philadelphia suburb, liked to sit on his back porch and smoke a cigar after his four-year-old son, Jake, went to sleep. His wife didn't seem to mind. After all, she liked to unwind at that time of night in her own way, which meant curling up on the couch in front of the TV.

One night, as Joe was sitting on the porch, he happened to look up at his son's second-floor window. To his surprise, he saw someone walking around in the boy's room. It couldn't have been Joe's wife because it looked like a man rather than a woman. And besides, Joe's wife was sitting on the couch, so she couldn't have been upstairs at the same time.

Putting down his cigar, Joe rushed upstairs to see what

was going on. But when he got there, the only person in the room was Jake. And though the boy was still half-awake, he didn't look the least bit frightened. In fact, as he lay under his covers, he seemed if anything more at ease than usual.

Yet Joe was stone-cold certain he had glimpsed an intruder. The next night, when he went out to the porch to smoke his cigar, he kept a watchful eye on his son's window. However, he didn't see a thing the whole time he was out there. He told himself that his sighting the previous night had been his imagination.

But the following evening, he saw it again—the figure of a man walking past Jake's window. As before, he sprinted up the stairs. And as before, he found his son dozing peacefully, looking calm and secure.

And alone.

It was a mystery, and Joe didn't like mysteries. Being an IT exec, he was used to dealing with things that could be identified and dealt with. He wasn't accustomed to experiences that couldn't be explained.

Joe's wife couldn't shed any light on the incidents. She hadn't seen an intruder, either in Jake's room or anywhere else in the house. However, the possibility of a stranger's invading their home obviously bothered her, too.

Though it was against his nature, Joe suggested to his wife that they should consult a paranormal investigator, and his search led him to T.A.P.S. Knowing a child was involved, Jason and I drove down to see the Tandys as soon as we possibly could. Being parents ourselves, we always feel a special sense of urgency in cases that affect kids.

The Tandys seemed like a nice-enough couple. However, both Jason and I thought we saw the occasional pot shot, mostly from Joe. Not having met them until that evening, we couldn't tell if their little gibes were meant to be jokes or if they were indicative of something more serious.

Jake, we discovered, was in the habit of sleeping on a mattress on his floor, rather than in his bed. We were told that he had anxiety issues that kept him awake at night. However, his parents didn't seem eager to elaborate on them, so we didn't push for more information.

In any case, we conducted an investigation of the premises. We placed cameras in Jake's room and elsewhere in the house and sat with Joe on his porch to see if the figure he had described made an appearance. Unfortunately, there was no sign of it, either from the porch or on the videotape we recorded and later reviewed.

Joe, in particular, was disappointed that we hadn't found anything. However, he understood that the scope of our investigation was limited by the amount of time we could devote to it. And whether we had discovered anything or not, he believed in what he had seen.

In the meantime, it turned out that Joe's family had other issues. He once believed that he had married a wonderful woman, someone who would be not only a great wife but also a great mother to their children. But little by little, he was discovering that his wife wasn't the person he thought she was.

At first, Joe only saw a few incidents of verbal abuse—the way his wife called their son a "retard" when he had an accident, the way she yelled at him when he got his clothes dirty, the threats she made when he broke something in the house. Those things were bad enough. Then Joe realized there was more to it.

His wife began spanking the boy for everything he did wrong. On one occasion, he came home from work and saw welts on Jake's face, left there by Jake's mother after the boy talked back to her. Gradually, it occurred to Joe that these things had happened before. He just hadn't been aware of it.

He began to have words with his wife. *Heated* words. He told her that she had to stop hitting Jake, that it wasn't right. She said that Joe would hit Jake, too, if he had to spend the whole day with him.

Joe was always on the verge of calling the police, but never followed through. Instead, he got a lawyer and petitioned a judge for a divorce. His wife, who was at the end of her rope, didn't fight the idea very much.

A year later, Joe and his wife were divorced. In the settlement, he managed to get the house. He also received custody of his son, which had been his main objective throughout the proceedings.

Jason and I had occasion to speak with Joe several times after we completed our investigation. We were surprised to hear about his separation from his wife, and about their divorce. As I said, they seemed like a nice couple.

"And the activity?" I asked.

"Gone," he said. "I haven't seen a hint of the figure since my wife left. And I think I know why."

His theory was that the figure had appeared to protect Jake from his mother's abuse. That's why the boy always looked so peaceful when Joe came into the room after a sighting—because Jake knew he was safe from his mother as long as the figure was around.

It made sense, in a way. Joe had had a feeling that his wife wasn't treating Jake right, but couldn't verify his suspicions. The figure could have been a subconscious manifestation of Joe's concerns, appearing in Jake's room to do what Joe would have done if he were sure about his wife's behavior.

That is, if there was a figure at all. And if the boy's mother was indeed abusing him on a regular basis. And if Joe wasn't making it all up. In the absence of any tangible evidence, his word was the only thing we had to go on.

One thing was for sure—Jake seemed a whole lot happier after the divorce. So maybe there was something to Joe's story after all.

GHOST HUNTER'S MANUAL: GOOD...OR EVIL?

One of the first questions people ask themselves when they're confronted with paranormal activity is, "Is it good or is it evil?" All too frequently, they tell themselves, "Of course it's evil, it just slammed a door!"

This is an attitude that comes from watching too many scary movies and listening to too many ghost stories around the fire. In our society, ghosts are associated with evil. There's no denying that, no getting around it. But in fact, the spirits of the dead are seldom out to do anyone harm.

Just because they're ghostly doesn't mean they're evil.

For one thing, the spirits most people encounter in their homes are human spirits, who were once as alive as you or I. They were born on earth. They had parents, grandparents, great-grandparents. Maybe siblings. More than likely, they had mortgages to pay off, bosses to deal with. They had wives, kids, neighbors, and friends.

You've got a dog? A cat? Maybe a couple of goldfish? So did these human spirits, once upon a time. Of course, that ended when they died. But until then, they were just like the rest of us.

For one of many reasons, which we discuss elsewhere in this book, they are still hanging around. But they didn't all suddenly develop the same personality, the same attitude. Their outlooks are as varied after death as they were when they were alive. Sure, some of them are cranky by nature, or jealous, or spiteful. But others are generous and giving, and still others love nothing more than a good laugh.

One spirit could be a loving grandmother simply looking for her husband. Another could be a teenage punk who's getting a kick out of scaring you. Get the idea? Anything is possible.

Fortunately the majority of us humans tend to be rather decent folks. So when we're investigating a suspected haunting, we at T.A.P.S. keep an open mind. We judge a spirit by how it acts, the same way we judge the living.

Of course, we sometimes come across inhuman entities—the kind that never lived on earth. They're always bad news.

But they're rare, as spirits go, and we'd never judge all spirits by the few bad apples in their midst.

Maybe the most important thing to consider when dealing with spirits is that one day we'll be dead as well. And maybe we'll have reasons to hang back, to want to remain in the world of the living. In that case, would we want the living to think of us all as uniformly evil?

It's something to think about.

Jason:
The Swinging Gate

1997

Sandy and David Van Horn had moved to Hackensack, New Jersey, just before Christmas 1996. Their house was the kind of home they had always dreamed of owning, a raised ranch with a nice pool in the backyard so they could cool off on hot summer days and barbecue beside it on summer nights. They had every expectation of enjoying their new home for many years to come.

What they didn't expect was to be searching the internet for paranormal investigators months later—which was how they found T.A.P.S., and why we soon found ourselves packing up the van for another investigation.

Four of us made the trip down to Hackensack, Brittney and Ed as well as Grant and myself. We got down there in the middle of the afternoon. It was late November, almost

Thanksgiving. At that time of year, you get warm days and cold ones. This was one of the cold ones.

The Van Horns turned out to be a nice couple in their midthirties, the kind we could easily have invited to our homes for dinner. Their daughter, Erin, was also very nice. But it was clear that something was troubling them. We asked Sandy and David to elaborate on what they had told us over the phone.

They said that for the last nine months or so—pretty much since the day they moved into the house—strange things had been happening. "Most of them to *me*," David told us. He recalled for us one time when he and Sandy had gone to the supermarket and come home with their arms full of groceries.

Sandy had unlocked the door with her key. But before she could push it open, it swung aside as if on its own. At the time, neither she nor David gave it a second thought. But as soon as she was inside, and David was about to follow, the door swung closed again—so hard that it jarred his elbow and forced him to spill some of the groceries on the ground.

Still, neither of them worried about it. Until it happened again the next day, and again the day after that. In fact, it got to be an all-too-predictable pattern. The front door would open for Sandy and then close again after she went inside, as if it wanted nothing more than to make her life easier. David, on the other hand, had to open the door himself, and when he did it invariably slammed in his face. It broke three of his fingers on one occasion and caused him to hurt his ankle on another.

Obviously, Sandy wasn't happy about her husband's misfortunes. But what really shook her up were the sounds she kept hearing of kids playing in her pool, laughing and yelling and generally having a good time. In the summertime, such sounds would have been a matter of no small concern, because kids can hurt themselves in a pool—especially without adults around to provide supervision.

But far from being summer, it was late fall. The temperatures were already near freezing. It would have been crazy for any of the neighborhood kids to jump Sandy's chain-link fence and go for a swim.

It was especially crazy because the pool was covered with a tarpaulin and had been drained for the winter. There was no water to swim in, for godsakes. Yet she kept hearing the sounds, as clear as day.

As a result, Sandy found herself constantly going outside to make sure no one was in the pool. Of course, she didn't see anyone. But after she went back inside, she heard the sounds again. It was making her a nervous wreck. Having a child of her own, she was especially sensitive to the issue of child safety.

There had been other occurrences as well. For instance, the rocking chair in the living room had been seen rocking on its own. And one time a light was observed flitting down the hallway and then disappearing into Erin's room.

We assured the Van Horns that we would do everything we could to determine the cause of their problems. That seemed to be of some comfort to them. On the other hand, they understood that we weren't making any promises.

Knowing we would have to cover multiple locations, we had brought four video cameras with us from Rhode

Island. Grant set one up on the ground floor of the house, training it on the rocking chair. A second camera was positioned to shoot down the hallway into Erin's room. A third covered the kitchen area, especially the back door, and a fourth was pointed in the direction of the pool.

Sometimes Grant and I stay to talk with our clients and let our associates take care of the equipment. Other times we lend a hand. It really depends on who we have with us and the complexity of the setup. In this case, we were all involved in transporting equipment, all going back and forth from our van to the house through the gate that opened into the Van Horns' backyard.

At one point, I went out to grab a power supply adaptor for one of our cameras. I had to pass through the gate to get out to the street, and then again to re-enter the backyard. But as I went through the opening the second time, the gate swung back at me.

That's interesting, I thought.

There was no wind to speak of, not even a breeze. The gate hadn't been built on an incline, where gravity might have pulled it closed. Had I, without thinking, pushed it too hard and caused it to recoil?

I didn't believe so. But just to make sure, I pushed it open again very gradually and deliberately. There was no resistance, nothing pushing back. When the gate had opened far enough to accommodate me, I tried to go through again.

And again it swung closed on me.

I had never in my life been so glad that I'd set up a camera in a particular place. Sometimes amazing things happen in the course of our investigations and we curse ourselves for not having gotten video evidence. In this case, we had captured the entire incident on tape.

But I wasn't satisfied. As Grant will tell you, I never am. I wanted to see if my colleagues had the same experience I did. So one by one, I asked them to get me something from the van.

The gate swung closed on each of them, the same way it did on me. It closed on Grant hardest of all, giving him a nice shot in the knee. He was a little miffed when I told him afterward that I knew it would happen, but he understood where I was coming from. Anything in the name of science.

We also caught video evidence of activity inside the house. One camera showed us a shadowy object that flew by very quickly, turned a corner, and shot up a staircase. If we had been outside and it had moved more slowly, I would have said it was a bat. As it was, we couldn't explain it.

Another camera showed us a point of white light that suddenly came into view and took off down a hallway into Erin's room. We tried hard to formulate an explanation for it, but failed to do so. There wasn't any source of either radiated or reflected light that could have been responsible for the phenomenon.

As far as we could tell, there was no activity by the back door. The rocking chair didn't move either. Grant and I watched both areas on and off the entire night, but to no avail.

At about four in the morning, we decided to call it quits. But by then, we had seen enough to know what we were dealing with. We thanked the Van Horns for their hospitality and told them we would be in touch as soon as we'd had a chance to review our data.

All the way back up to Rhode Island, Grant and I talked about the gate that had swung closed on me, and then on him. It wasn't that doors hadn't closed on us before. It was just that this time we had gotten such a clear-cut shot of it.

"A nice piece of evidence," said my partner, nodding with satisfaction.

"One of several," I said, thinking of the bat shadow that went up the stairs and the lights that shot down the hall-way.

Back home, we watched the footage of the gate closing. Not just once, but over and over again. It was almost as re-markable seeing it in a recording as it was experiencing it in person.

When we contacted the Van Horns to tell them about our findings, they were eager to hear what we had to say. In fact, as eager as any client we had ever had. We were glad to be able to say there was a reason for the problems they had encountered.

"In our opinion," I told them, "you've got some definite paranormal activity taking place in and around your house. More specifically, a human spirit." I explained to them what that meant—that it was the spiritual remains of what had been a human being at one time.

"What can we do about it?" David asked.

"It was a person once," I told him, "so the best strategy is to reason with it. Tell it you don't mind it helping your wife when you're not around, but when you're in the house it's got to make itself scarce. Otherwise, you'll bring in some-body to make it leave altogether."

Of course, no one can force a human spirit to depart if it doesn't want to. However, there are sensitives who know how to harass it to the point where it can't stand the thought of remaining.

Fortunately, that wasn't necessary in this case. David had a conversation with the spirit and came to an agreement with it. As far as we know, it hasn't bothered him or his family since.

GHOST HUNTER'S MANUAL: EVIDENCE

Jason has a saying that describes our philosophy when it comes to paranormal investigation: "If you set out to prove a haunting, anything will seem like evidence. If you set out to disprove it, you'll end up with only those things you can't explain away."

At T.A.P.S., those are the words we live by every time we set up our video cameras in a client's house. It's not our intention to back up anyone's claim that something supernatural is taking place. We let other groups do that. Our objective, first, last, and always, is to debunk.

Debunking, as the dictionary will tell you, is the art of exposing claims as pretentious, false, or exaggerated—in other words, taking the "bunk" out. Bunk, in turn, comes from "bunkum," which is speech that lacks substance. As paranormal investigators, we shine a light on claims that may be false or exaggerated; using a scientific approach, we check for substance.

Most of the time—in fact, in about 80 percent of the

cases we take on—we don't *find* any substance. We attribute what other people claim is proof of the supernatural to thoroughly natural causes. What's more, we get a kick out of it. Truth be told, we like finding mundane explanations for seemingly inexplicable events.

It's only in the other 20 percent of our cases, the ones where we can't find an explanation, that we admit the possibility of the paranormal. And, of course, we get a kick out of those as well. But before we can concede there's something ghostly going on, we've got to make sure of our evidence.

We much prefer the kind that can be examined by others. That means photographs, video recordings, and audio recordings, because other people can go over them and come to the same conclusions we did. But before we show the evidence to them, we run it through some rigorous tests of our own.

We ask ourselves if some naturally occurring condition could have created the noise, image, or sensation in question. Was the cold spot in the attic a sign of a spirit manifesting or just a draft through a broken window? Was the banging in the basement the product of a cranky ghost or a cranky heating pipe? If there's any doubt whatsoever, we withhold our verdict until we dispel it.

That's one reason we've developed a reputation for integrity in our field. We're more skeptical about our evidence than other people are. We consistently hold ourselves to a higher standard.

Which is why when we find something suspicious, we subject it to as many different kinds of analysis as possible. If we pick up a bunch of EVPs in one part of a house, we see if we can obtain a video image as well. If our digital thermometers indicate a drastic rise in temperature, we subject the area to more intense scrutiny with our infrared cameras. And so on.

Personal experiences aren't as good as documentation, because they can't be examined by people who weren't present when the incident occurred. But when they're reported by two people at the same time, they carry some weight. That's why we always try to have our investigators work in pairs—so if one of them makes a claim, the other one can back him up.

One mistake a lot of newbie ghost hunters make is allowing the client to become part of the investigation. Let's be very clear about this—you work on behalf of your clients, you don't work *with* them. Otherwise, you can't say for certain that your evidence isn't tainted.

After all, your client believes—or at least suspects—that his house is haunted. Consciously or unconsciously, he's probably looking for proof of it. Do you really want to give someone with that kind of agenda access to your cameras and your other recording devices? Or even let him in on your team discussions?

At T.A.P.S., we keep our clients as far away from the investigation as possible. We never leave them alone with our equipment. And we don't present our findings to them until we've had ample time to analyze our data.

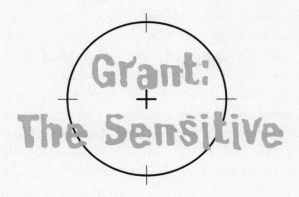

Grant: The Sensitive

1997

Lisa Cabrini and her husband were living in a small house on a back road in western Massachusetts. She was in her late forties or early fifties, with bright orange hair. Many of our clients are at their wits' end when we arrive, fearful for their sanity. Lisa was no exception. She didn't know what was going on and it scared her.

Her husband, on the other hand, didn't seem the least bit alarmed. He told us that he hadn't experienced anything unusual in the house or anywhere else, and that he didn't take much stock in his wife's claims. In fact, he sat and read the newspaper almost the entire time we were there.

Sitting down with Lisa in her kitchen, we asked her to tell us what was happening in her home. The first thing she said was that she believed she was becoming a sensitive.

At least, that was the conclusion her friends had reached when she told them what was happening.

We hear that kind of thing a lot—that people feel they're becoming attuned to paranormal phenomena in some way. In fact, true sensitives are few and very far between, so we always reserve comment on that count.

Lisa told us that she had seen ghostly entities in her house, pretty much all over the place. She had even tried to photograph them, to no avail. When we asked her to be more specific about her experiences, she said that she had seen objects like coffee cups and books flying from room to room. On hearing that, Jason and I looked at each other. In movies, ghosts are often seen flying around a room. In real life, that doesn't happen—at least not in our experience.

The "flying" remark immediately made us more skeptical about Lisa's claims. We asked her if she was on any form of medication, which she was. Two of them, in fact. However, when we looked them up, we didn't see anything about them that might give rise to hallucinations.

Our next step was to research the house and the surrounding area, looking for anything that might explain why her house might be haunted. We took photos, made recordings, and left ourselves open to personal experiences, but nothing turned up. Not even a limestone deposit, which is often a factor in residual hauntings, since limestone seems to store paranormal energies.

We had asked for permission to go through Lisa's drawers and cabinets, though we exploited this permission only on a limited basis. Even when clients give us carte blanche, we try to avoid violating their privacy whenever possible.

This time when we went back, we checked out her medicine cabinet—and found some prescriptions she hadn't mentioned in her conversations with us.

We looked them up and found that one in particular, if mixed with a prescription she *had* mentioned, resulted in a hallucinogen. We brought this to her attention. She confessed that she had indeed mixed her current prescription with the older one, not just once but on several occasions.

Convinced that this was the problem, we advised her to talk with her doctor. He gave her a new prescription that didn't have the same side effects. All of a sudden, the ghosts in her house disappeared.

GHOST HUNTER'S MANUAL: PHOTOGRAPHS

You'd be surprised how many potentially eye-popping shots of paranormal phenomena have been ruined or discredited because the photographer neglected to observe the most basic rules of photography.

Maybe he let his camera strap get in the way of the picture. Maybe he caught a wisp of somebody's frozen breath on a cold winter's day. Maybe he just forgot to clean the fingerprints off his lens from the night before. No matter the reason, he missed an opportunity to capture an apparition for posterity.

If you were taking pictures of a wedding, you'd want them to be clear and unobstructed, wouldn't you? Then why not take the same care with your investigative photos? In either case, you're taking pictures of something that you'll never have an opportunity to see again.

Steve Gonsalves, one of the mainstays of the T.A.P.S. organization and our TV investigations as well, likes to emphasize the use of control pictures. These are pictures of a nonparanormal nature on the same roll of film with pictures of a paranormal nature. The nonparanormal shots show what kind of image the camera takes when there's no supernatural activity around.

That way, when one of the pictures on the roll shows suspicious activity, no one can say it was the camera or the film that caused the anomaly. After all, you have proof to the contrary. When scientists run experiments, they use control groups to isolate certain variables. That's what we do when we take control pictures.

For instance, let's say you're investigating a case in which the client has seen activity in a certain room. You want to take some pictures of that room to show what it looks like under normal circumstances. Later, if you take some pictures of the same spot and there's a misty image in them, you can say with some confidence that you've captured evidence of something supernatural.

The key is to be as professional as possible. But then, that's true of all aspects of paranormal investigation. A little care and forethought go a long way.

Jason:
Demon

1997

G rant and I never underestimate the spirits we deal with, especially when it appears to us that they may be malevolent, or what those of us involved with the paranormal would call *inhuman*. We know it's possible to feel safe one moment and find ourselves in deadly danger the next, so we take every precaution we possibly can. But sometimes even the most thorough precautions aren't enough, and we can't keep an entity from claiming an innocent victim.

From the moment we set foot in the Mason residence, a two-bedroom basement apartment in central Rhode Island, we had the feeling that we were dealing with an inhuman haunting. Even the clergymen who had visited the home in recent weeks had told the family that they felt uncomfortable there.

For some who call themselves paranormal investigators, that feeling would be enough. They would pronounce the place haunted, no question about it. Grant and I depend on our feelings, but we know we have to back them up with hard evidence if our work and the overall field of ghost-hunting are ever to be taken seriously.

Our clients in this case, the Masons, were understandably terrified. All three of them had had disturbing and even violent experiences. Gayle Mason had caught sight of dark shapes—what she believed were angry spirits—almost every night for the last month or so. Her husband, Will, had twice been awakened at three in the morning by what felt like a punch in the face. And their two-year-old daughter, Melanie, had taken to hiding under her blanket and screaming "No!" in response to the voices she heard, which suggested she do "terrible things."

Three of us made the trip to the Mason place in the middle of October. In this case, Grant and I had brought along Tevor Lions, a Protestant priest with a talent for exorcising unwanted supernatural entities. We had a feeling we would need his services before the night was through.

We arrived at the house in the evening, pulling up into a driveway full of fallen leaves. It had been a cold, wet day, and there was more of the same in the forecast.

Melanie, we were told, had just gone to bed. While Grant interviewed Will and Gayle, Tevor and I took a look around. In the course of my search, I found several horror movies, but nothing else that might have set the stage for a supernatural intruder. No Ouija boards, books about devil worship, or other signs of involvement with the occult, which we sometimes come across when we're dealing with an inhuman spirit.

Will and Gayle admitted to having recently watched *The Amityville Horror,* a movie about a wildly violent inhuman haunting on Long Island. However, they had turned it off halfway through because of the ominous feeling that seemed to have pervaded the room and Melanie's waking up crying. Neither of them had watched anything even remotely frightening since.

It didn't take us long to set up our equipment, since we were dealing with a relatively simple residence—just a living room, a kitchen, and a bathroom in addition to the bedrooms. At eleven o'clock, Will said he had to call it a night. Apparently, he had an early morning at work the next day.

I'm not sure he would have gone to bed so easily if Grant and I hadn't been there. Both he and his wife seemed to find comfort in our presence. For our part, we didn't want to disappoint them.

At about one-thirty in the morning, I was sitting in the living room with Gayle, listening to her describe some of her experiences, when I saw her eyes suddenly go wide. Looking back over my shoulder, I saw what had alarmed her. There was a dark mass moving through the kitchen in the direction of the bedrooms.

Gayle stifled a scream as I got up and went after the mass. But a second later, it was gone. We conducted an extensive search, but there was no sign of it in the bedrooms or anywhere else.

Around 2:45 A.M., Melanie woke up crying, complaining that something or someone was bothering her. Gayle came out with Melanie in her arms and said that the child's room smelled awful. When Grant and I checked it out, we encountered an overpowering stench like that of feces. But Melanie wasn't responsible for it. She was potty-trained, and there was no indication that she had had an accident.

As we stood there in Melanie's bedroom, the temperature around us increased dramatically. Our thermometer showed a difference of eight degrees, and our EMF detector spiked, indicating the kind of sharp leap in ambient energy that often accompanies a paranormal event.

By then, Gayle had returned to Melanie's room, but we ushered her out again. A moment later, the door to the master bedroom slammed shut. When Grant and I went to investigate, we saw Will emerge from the room. He looked completely disoriented, his eyes glassy and unfocused. Before we could ask him what was wrong, he growled from deep in his throat that he was going to beat the hell out of us. Then he lunged at us, fists flying, as if we were a danger to his family.

We understood that Will was out of control and didn't want to hurt him if we could help it, but we also didn't want to sustain any serious injuries ourselves. What's more, in his confused condition, he represented a threat to his wife and daughter. We had to take that into account as well.

Though he was a big fellow and he was swinging wildly, Grant and I managed to keep him boxed in without absorbing any really bad punches. But only for a while. Then he got past us and starting throwing things, household objects, whatever he could get his hands on. His wife screamed at him, imploring him to stop, but it had no effect.

Before we could stop him, Will ripped the phone right out of the wall. Then he turned on us, yelling nonsense riddled with vulgarity. Grant and I stood our ground, hoping he wouldn't make a move to hurt Gayle or Melanie.

In the meantime, Tevor began saying prayers, directing them at Will but really addressing the entity that was afflicting him. Will's face became a battlefield, a struggle between Tevor's religious provocation and the inhuman power that had invaded the Masons' apartment. For a moment, it wasn't clear to me which of them would come out on top.

Then the wild look in Will's eyes started to fade. Little by little, his rage ebbed away. Finally, he stumbled back into his bedroom and collapsed on the bed.

We followed him in to make sure he was okay. Will looked dazed and weak, his chest heaving as if he had just run a marathon. He didn't remember any of what he had done. However, the phone he had ripped out of the wall, which was now lying on the kitchen floor, was a testament that something had taken place.

Tevor asked Gayle if she wanted him to bless her home. After all, whatever had gotten into Will was still present. She told him to go ahead, and he did. It took a while for Tevor to say all the necessary prayers, but eventually the apartment was cleansed.

No further activity ensued that night, and the family was grateful—Will in particular. In fact, he couldn't thank us enough. As far as T.A.P.S. was concerned, we were happy to help. We believed that we had gotten rid of the inhuman entity plaguing the Masons.

But the morning after we left, in the house across the street, a woman went out of her mind and shot her husband. So maybe, despite our best efforts, we were not as successful as we had thought.

Jason: Invader

1998

Pat Bozelle's dread was evident in his voice when he said, "I hear someone in our house!"

Even in our early days, we were getting a lot of calls from concerned homeowners about the possibility of paranormal phenomena on their properties. But this guy on the phone seemed more than just concerned. He sounded frightened to death. He told us that he had called the police on several occasions, and that they had come over each time and dutifully conducted a search of the area. Unfortunately, none of their efforts had turned up evidence of an intruder.

We told Pat that we would drive up to the town in Maine where he lived and see if we could help him. But first we made a phone call, looking for some perspective. Luckily, one of our friends—a uniformed officer in Warwick, Rhode Island—had a connection to a detective in Pat's local police department. The detective confirmed what Pat had told us: The police had been out to the Bozelle property four times over the last few months, but they hadn't found the slightest sign of anything amiss. The police had come to believe that Pat had an overactive imagination and was looking for attention. Nonetheless, we had promised Pat that we would take a look around, so we packed up our equipment for a trip to Maine.

Our team consisted of Grant, me, an investigator we had worked with before named Cole Morris, and Ed Gaines. We took off from Rhode Island in the late morning of Saturday, June 6, and arrived at the Bozelle place about 4:00 P.M. Pat and his wife, Teri, who were both in their midthirties, were there to greet us.

They had two children, nine-year-old Patrick Jr. and six-year-old Aileen. Sitting down with us in his living room, Pat repeated what he had told us on the phone—that he had heard someone in his house late at night, walking around and making noises that frightened Pat's family. Yet whenever he got out of bed and went looking for the intruder, he found no one there.

When we interviewed the family, we could see that they were all concerned for their safety. Everyone in the house had been awakened at one time or another by disturbing sounds, which included screams, banging noises, and the rattling of their bedroom door handles as if someone were about to enter their rooms. The children said they often hid under the covers in fear.

It appeared to us that the family was sincere in their belief that something was in their home. We don't like to see people suffer, regardless of the reason for it, so we proceeded with our investigation.

By 8:15 P.M., we had finished setting up our equipment, which consisted of four camcorders, four cassette recorders, and three ambient thermometers. At 10:00 P.M., Pat and Teri put their children to bed. Up to that point, we hadn't detected any unusual activity. When the clock struck midnight, things were still peaceful. I recalled what the local police had said about Pat's having an overactive imagination, and started to wonder if they weren't right.

On the other hand, we had been through plenty of investigations where the action didn't get underway until the wee hours of the morning. Only time would tell.

At 1:30 A.M., we heard banging sounds coming from the basement. Grant and I looked at each other, thinking the same thought at the same time: We had heard that kind of banging before, and it didn't represent a supernatural event. When we traced the sound to its source, we found that one of the pipes that fed the boiler was loose and was banging on the floor joist.

Grant and I are plumbers at heart. We're as fascinated, sometimes, by what goes wrong in a house as we are by the paranormal. What's more, we usually know how to fix anything in need of repair. Securing the Bozelles' loose boiler pipe was one of the easier jobs we had ever done for a client.

Once we took care of the repair, the house fell quiet again. As the night wore on, I began to believe we had debunked Pat's claims, which, of course, was an accomplishment in itself. Not every T.A.P.S. investigation leads to evidence of a haunting. In fact, very few of them do.

In any case, we weren't going to jump to any conclusions. We had made the trip up to Maine for a reason, and we were going to see the investigation through. Cleaning up from our repair job, we hunkered down and waited.

At about 2:45 A.M., we heard a loud screeching noise from outside the house. Rushing out, we looked around with our flashlights but didn't see anything. Chalking it up to an animal in the woods behind the house, we went back inside.

By three-thirty, we were getting antsy and decided to walk around outside—not just Grant and me, but Ed and Cole as well. As we stood there, we discussed the possibility of the Bozelles' claims being based on animal noises, maybe coming from the attic if an animal had figured out how to get in there. Considering the absence of any other evidence, that seemed the most likely explanation.

Then, maybe twenty minutes after we went outside, we heard a loud scream from inside the house. It wasn't the kind of scream you might hear from an animal. It was human, and bloodcurdling.

We tried to get back inside through the door we had left by, but it was locked and we couldn't re-enter without breaking it. Again, we heard a scream—more than one, in fact. They sounded like a man caught in the grip of terror. And there were bangs, too loud to be a recurrence of the loose boiler pipe.

Running around the perimeter of the house, we tried the back door, but that was locked as well. Finally, we went over to Pat and Teri's bedroom window and knocked on it, waving our flashlight beams through the window for good measure.

Our knocking surprised them, but not as much as the sounds inside their house. In fact, they were already sitting up in bed, scared half to death. Opening the window, they let Grant and me climb inside.

We heard the doorknob rattle as if someone were trying to get in, just as Pat had described to us. Swinging open the bedroom door, we peered outside into the darkened hallway. If there was something out there, we wanted to catch a glimpse of it.

But we didn't see anything. And as soon as the door was open, all the sounds stopped. Our next thought, and that of the Bozelles, was for the children. Checking on them, we saw that they were both awake and hiding under their covers.

Only then did we remember that Ed and Cole were still outside. Opening the front door, we let them back in and told them what we had experienced. How the door became locked was something we couldn't explain, since we've learned over the years to be careful about locking doors behind us.

Nothing else happened that night. When the sun comes up, we usually pack our equipment and head for home. This time was an exception. We lingered at the Bozelle place until about two in the afternoon, feeling there was more we could do there. But for the time being, we had done all we could.

Grant and I headed back to Rhode Island, but Ed and Cole stayed in town, and on Monday morning conducted some research at the local historical society. At three-thirty that afternoon, Ed called me collect from a pay phone outside town to tell me that he and Cole might have found something. They would be back in Rhode Island in a few hours to explain.

As soon as I hung up with Ed, I called Grant and asked him to come over. Both of us were burning with curiosity, wondering what our colleagues had unearthed. At 9:00 P.M., they pulled up in front of my house, and we all headed downstairs into the T.A.P.S. office I had set up there.

"I believe," said Cole, with a note of accomplishment in his voice, "we've figured out what's going on in the Bozelle house."

"Okay," I told him. "Lay it on us."

He did just that.

Back in 1864, there was a savage legal dispute over a parcel of land that included what had become the Bozelles' property and the abutting twenty-five acres. The sides involved in the struggle were the Adams family and the Abrahms family, who apparently hated each other like poison. Three weeks after the dispute wound up in the local courts, the patriarch of the Adams family was found in a pool of his own blood, the cause of death a pistol shot to the side of the head.

The murder weapon belonged to the victim, so the case was judged a suicide and closed. Of course, there were those who said that Old Man Abrahms had something to do with Adams's death, but the accusation remained just an accusation because no one could ever come up with proof.

If Adams's death had indeed come at the hands of Old Man Abrahms, the victim's spirit may have lingered in our world to take back his land. At 11:00 P.M., Grant and I called Pat Bozelle to tell him we had had a breakthrough. We told him that we would be heading back up to his house on Thursday.

At 7:00 P.M. on Thursday, Grant and I brought Mike Foley with us up to the Bozelles' house. Mike is a friend of ours and a self-proclaimed sensitive. He doesn't talk with people about his ability to sense supernatural entities, but he assists us from time to time on certain cases. He had agreed to join us on this one.

While Mike walked around the house, Grant and I sat down with the Bozelles in their living room to discuss what we had discovered about their property. Pat and Teri seemed surprised—but also relieved. After all, if we were right about Adams, the activity in the house was human and not demonic. On the other hand, they were still frightened for their family.

Around 8:30 P.M., Mike joined us in the living room and said he believed that Adams was present in the house. However, Adams was hanging back at the moment, watching and waiting. Mike asked for permission to go up to the attic on his own. Grant and I were reluctant to let him go it alone, but Mike insisted. Pat, who wanted desperately to get the entity out of his house, gave Mike access to the attic.

Pat and Teri put their children to bed just before nine o'clock. Grant and I, who were still sitting in the living room, could hear Mike talking up in the attic. His voice was getting stern, forceful. At nine-thirty, he came down from the attic to talk to the Bozelles and ask if he could stay the night. Pat and Teri looked at each other and agreed—anything to put an end to their ordeal. Grant and I decided to remain in the house as well, just in case we were needed.

At eleven-thirty, Mike went back up to the attic again while Grant and I stayed in the living room. As before, we could hear Mike speaking loudly and sternly, the way one might talk address a disobedient child. Suddenly, there were three loud bangs, one after the other. Grant and I didn't say anything—we just bolted up the stairs, toward the attic. On the way, we ran into Pat and Teri, who had been awakened by the banging sounds and were more than a little alarmed.

On entering the attic, we saw Mike sitting in an old camping chair he had found while he was up there. He was leaning forward, looking as pale and haggard as if he had just run a marathon. He gestured to us to stand still; we did just that.

We waited patiently to see what Mike was going to do next. For all we knew, he was going to call it a night. We certainly wouldn't have blamed him, considering the way he looked and what he must have gone through. But he wasn't done after all. As it turned out, he was just getting started.

Just before one o'clock in the morning, Mike started talking again. In a steady but insistent voice, he asked Adams to leave the Bozelles and their house alone. There was a loud bang from somewhere in the house as some boxes a few feet in front of Mike fell over, looking as if they intended to hit him. Then three more loud bangs. Then silence.

We looked at Mike, unable to tell from his expression whether he had been successful. Then he looked back at us and said, in reference to Adams, "He's leaving now. He's not happy, but he's leaving."

Still, we waited to see if there would be any more activity. There wasn't. Finally, at about 2:00 A.M., we decided to get some sleep. The rest of the night was uneventful in the Bozelles' house. At ten in the morning, we packed up our stuff, told Pat and Teri to stay in touch, and went home to Rhode Island.

Over the next few months, there were no reports of any paranormal activity. Last we heard, the Bozelles were happy to have their house back, and relieved to be able to sleep at night without being awakened by a restless spirit.

GHOST HUNTER'S MANUAL: DEALING WITH SPIRITS

The biggest mistake people make in trying to speak with a spirit is to look at the process strictly from their own point of view—and not from the spirit's. Anyone attempting to contact a supernatural entity wants to learn something, to obtain some information he or she can't get any other way. Often it concerns events for which the spirit seems to be responsible.

However, the spirit isn't always inclined to respond. After all, why should it? What does it have to gain by answering the questions of the living?

If you were in an unfamiliar part of town and you were asking directions, would you demand them of the first person you met? Of course not. You would be as polite as possible, because that person has no motivation to help you. If he or she does so, it's out of the goodness of his or her heart.

Dealing with spirits is something like that. To do so effectively, you have to keep in mind what they want—which, in most cases, is the attention of the living. They've remained in our world after death for a reason. They have an ax to grind, or they're seeking some kind of closure. If you're willing to at least acknowledge their agenda, they'll be more likely to help you with yours.

The other thing to keep in mind is that spirits are limited in how quickly and clearly they can respond to a question. It's not like talking to another living person, who may be just a few feet away. You're crossing a barrier of life and death, and the connection may be a little fuzzy.

With that in mind, make sure you're doing your best to be understood. Speak slowly and clearly, and do everything in your power to keep your emotions under wraps. After you pose a question, give the spirit a chance to consider it and compose an answer. The amount of time it requires will vary with the complexity of the question, among other factors, but a few seconds is a good rule of thumb.

What happens if you don't get a response? You might try framing your question a little differently. For instance, you might have asked, "Are you the one who's been moving the chairs?" If there's no reply, you might try asking, "Is there a spirit moving the chairs?" And then, a little later on, "Do you know who it is?"

Then again, your question may be one the spirit just

doesn't want to answer. In that case, you can ask it from now till Doomsday and you won't get a response. If you've framed your question a few different ways and you still haven't received an answer, move on. Ask something else.

Ultimately, what you want to do is establish a dialogue. But keep in mind that a spirit has other ways to respond besides intelligible speech. Sometimes a growl, a moving shadow, or a shove from an unseen hand can be a more eloquent answer to your question than a whispered word.

Grant:
Wild Claims

1999

Steve and Iris Westin lived in Smithfield, Rhode Island, a town of about twenty thousand people located eleven miles northwest of Providence. They lived in Smithfield because it was a quiet town, with relatively little commercial development and lots of heavily forested land in which to hike. There was also a seventy-five-acre wildlife preserve in the area, where any number of endangered species could find protection.

Smithfield was also an old community, founded in the 1600s. And like many old communities in New England, it boasted its share of supposed ghost sightings. Some people said they had seen men with grotesque animal heads. Others claimed they had seen women with no heads at all. Still others spoke of apparitions of people covered with blood or burning like candles.

Steve and Iris weren't what you would call believers in the supernatural. They were entertained by all the stories surrounding Smithfield, but they didn't put any particular stock in them. That is, until they began to have experiences in their home that gave them reason for concern.

For instance, there was the business about the lights. They flickered from time to time, as if something were sucking all the energy out of the electrical wires. The Westins had heard that that was a sign of ghostly activity.

Several times a day, especially at night, they heard a banging in the house's exterior walls. It sounded to them like the work of an angry spirit. And then there were the shrieks coming from the attic —thin, high-pitched wailings like someone screaming from far away.

In addition, Steve and Iris had the sense that they were being watched by someone. Or maybe by some*thing*. They were constantly looking back over their shoulders, expecting to see an intruder standing there.

From our headquarters in Warwick, it was a short drive up Route 295 to Smithfield. When we arrived, we sat down with the Westins and discussed their experiences in more detail. Then we set up our cameras and recorders in key locations and waited for something to happen.

Jason and I wound up investigating the house for two days running. We made plenty of audio and video recordings in that time, and plenty of discoveries. However, none of them had anything to do with the paranormal.

It turned out that the house was a haven for various forms of wildlife. The banging in the walls, for instance, was caused by squirrels taking refuge there. Thanks to the lack of insulation, they had plenty of room in which to gather.

The screaming in the attic was actually the cries of a hawk that had worked its way through the attic vent and created a home for itself. The hawk was also responsible for the flickering of the lights. As it entered the attic, it would brush against a wire that led down to a chandelier in the kitchen, causing the flow of electricity to the fixture to be temporarily interrupted.

Steve and Iris were relieved that we hadn't found any ghosts in their house, and that all they needed was a contractor to take care of their problems. However, they also seemed a little disappointed. After all, they wouldn't be adding to the supernatural lore of Smithfield, Rhode Island.

GHOST HUNTER'S MANUAL: SCOUTING IT OUT

If you were trying to come up with a foolproof prescription for personal injury, wouldn't it be something like "walking around in the dark, full of eagerness and anxiety, focused on catching a glimpse of something fleeting instead of watching where the heck you're going"?

Yeah. Something like that. And in fact, that's what usually ends up happening on a ghost hunt. You're nervous, maybe even downright scared. You can't wait to see something supernatural. And you're concentrating so hard on scanning the place through your camera's eyepiece that you don't see the nail point coming up through the floor, or the desk that's about to claim a piece of your hip, or the hanging light fixture that's just itching to leave its mark on your forehead.

Before you go on any hunt, you should be familiar with the lay of the land. That means visiting the site beforehand, and doing so while it's still light out. This will allow you to identify potential hazards that could turn a full night's worth of fruitful investigation into an even longer night listening to seventies music as you sit in the emergency room of the local hospital.

Then you'll know where the desk is, how low the light fixture hangs, and how many steps you can take before you reach the end of that walk-in closet. You'll be able to minimize or even eliminate potential hazards. But there's another good reason for scouting a venue in advance.

After all, you're there to hunt ghosts, right? Then you need a roadmap in your head alerting you to places where noises and drafts can arise, so when you hear or feel these things late at night, you'll be able to determine their cause. Without that map, you'll be jumping to all sorts of wrong conclusions.

Where are all the electrical outlets—especially the ones that really work? You're going to need them if you expect to operate all the state-of-the-art equipment you brought with you. It's a lot easier to find outlets in the daytime than it is at night, when a key piece of evidence may depend on your locating a viable source of power.

A visit during the day will also tell you about the neighborhood. For example, the "Trespassers Will Be Shot On Sight" sign, located just beyond your client's property line. It's good to know about that *before* you go chasing some mysterious, dark shape helter-skelter through the woods.

If you spot such a sign, speak to the owner of the property in advance of your investigation. Ask him if it's all right to cross his boundary line just that one time. The last thing you want to do is get shot at in the middle of your investigation, or have to explain to the police why you're trespassing at three in the morning.

So scout it out. Take cameras, pens, paper, and anything else that will help you plan your investigation with an eye to safety, accuracy, and efficiency. Try to pick out all the conditions you think are going to make your life difficult, and maybe they won't be obstacles after dark.

Ghost-hunting is a tricky business even when you're thoroughly prepared—that's just the nature of the beast. A lack of preparation makes it a whole lot trickier. And we would hate for you to miss that once-in-a-lifetime full-body apparition because you were busy pulling your foot out of a hole.

Jason: Jenny and Mike

2000

When we pulled into Reading, Massachusetts, your typical small New England town, we thought we were just looking for ghosts. Little did we know that what we found there would have a lasting effect on The Atlantic Paranormal Society as well as on us personally.

Most of our clients contact us through our website. Kristyn Gartland was no exception. She was looking for a local group to address the problems she was having, and she stumbled onto us.

Kristyn lived with her son in a three-story, aluminum-sided apartment building on Salem Street, a busy thoroughfare in Reading. She called us because of the experiences she'd had there lately, experiences that made her wonder if the place might be haunted. She wasn't the only one of the building's six tenants who had had such experiences, either, though not all of them were as willing to talk about them as she was.

On this occasion, I brought two investigators, Ed and Brittney. Grant would have been there except his wife was giving birth at the time. Brittney sat down with Kristyn while Ed and I walked through the place, looking for places to set up our equipment. Unlike many of our clients, Kristyn wasn't freaked out by her experiences, bizarre as they had been. She was just concerned about her son's welfare and, of course, her own.

In the course of our interview, Kristyn told us that she had seen apparitions of people in her apartment on any number of occasions. It was hard to see their faces because they were so often running from room to room, but it seemed that two of them showed up over and over again—a boy and a girl.

Soon afterward, she discovered that her son had a couple of invisible friends. One, whom he called Jenny, was protective, almost motherly. The other one, whom he knew as Mike, was completely the opposite. Kristyn's son told her that Mike had threatened him with bodily harm if he didn't do what Mike wanted.

Kristyn also heard noises in the apartment, mostly at night. Many times they sounded like voices, the kind one might associate with children. Naturally, Kristyn wondered if there was a connection between the voices, the apparitions she had glimpsed, and her son's unseen companions.

Hence her decision to reach out to T.A.P.S.

We showed up with our video cameras, audio recorders, EMF meters, and digital thermometers. Kristyn's apartment was compact, so it didn't take long to set up. When we were done, we waited to see what the night would bring.

We didn't have to wait long before we came across evidence of Kristyn's claims. First, starting in the kitchen, we encountered abrupt increases in temperature. The baseline in the apartment was about sixty-seven degrees, but it jumped more than ten degrees in some places. We made a note of each fluctuation and went on.

Later in the night, we heard voices. Not just me alone, but our entire team. The voices seemed to come not from one spot but from everywhere at once, and we couldn't tell if they were male or female.

Still later, we saw globules of light, if only out of the corners of our eyes. They were small and round and bright, and they moved around a lot. Whenever we thought we could turn our heads and get a good look at them, they slipped away and eluded us.

And that was just what happened the first night. When we came back a second time, we had other experiences. First there was a banging sound like loud, metallic footsteps, which echoed throughout the apartment. But when we tried to find their source, we came up empty-handed.

Some time later, a couple of our investigators began to feel nauseated. They hadn't eaten the same food or been sitting in the same part of the apartment, so that couldn't be the answer. And the rest of us felt fine, so it was kind of a mystery.

We were still puzzling over it when, without warning, the bric-a-brac on Kristyn's walls began to shake. It looked as if they were caught in the middle of an earthquake. Yet none of us felt any vibration, either in the floor or anywhere else.

But the most compelling evidence of paranormal activity that we encountered that night was a dark mass roaming through Kristyn's apartment. It started in the kitchen, went out into the hall, and finally wound up in a bedroom. Fortunately, we managed to get off a series of photos before it disappeared into the woodwork.

Later on, we reviewed the photographs and saw the dark mass. It seemed to be growing in size from one photo to the next. This was the kind of evidence we always hope for, but seldom obtain.

Clearly, something of a supernatural nature had invaded the place. As for what might be at the root of it, Kristyn confessed that she had used a Ouija board in a casual attempt to contact the spirit world.

But it seemed to us there was more to the explanation. After all, there were at least two entities involved, Jenny and Mike—and Jenny, from all accounts, was benign. Mike, on the other hand, was an inhuman entity, judging by the threats he had made to Kristyn's son. Based on our experiences in other investigations, we guessed that the dark mass was a manifestation of Mike rather than Jenny.

However, we needed to know more. Mike could have entered the picture via Kristyn's Ouija board. But what was Jenny, who was probably a human spirit, doing there? Kristyn, who wasn't the type to stand around while other people labored on her behalf, offered to research the matter on her own.

She spoke with her landlord, who had lived in Reading all his life. She also spoke with other longtime residents of the town. What she discovered was chilling, without a doubt, but it also made sense.

Apparently, the apartment house in which Kristyn had taken up residence had a grisly history. It had been built on the grounds of an old cemetery, one that dated all the way back to the 1600s. The area's earliest residents, children as well as adults, had all been buried there.

The builders of the apartment house had done their best to remove all the cemetery's coffins and relocate them to a newer facility across the street. However, the coffins were made of pine, which had to have rotted over the years, making it unlikely that all the coffins had been removed intact. More than likely, there were still bones and debris left in the ground underneath the foundation.

When Kristyn visited the cemetery, which was right across Salem Street, she found one headstone that had just a single name on it: Jenny. The dates on the stone suggested that the person beneath it had died as a child. Was this Jenny the one whose spirit had taken hold in Kristyn's apartment?

With the dark mass in mind, Kristyn made the decision to have her home cleansed through religious provocation. We asked a priest of our acquaintance to conduct the ritual. However, he had barely gotten halfway through it before we heard screaming in the building, as if someone were in terrible pain. Outside Kristyn's apartment, on the stairway, there were long, deep-throated growls, loud enough to be heard clearly through her door.

Suddenly we heard the growls *inside* the apartment as well. They seemed to be coming from all around us, making the air shiver with their ferocity. Obviously, the demonic entity wasn't going to give up without a fight.

Then it all stopped. There was a big, empty silence. Peace.

At least for a while. After we left, Kristyn called us to say the worst of the activity had started up again. We had to go back a third time before we finally cleansed the place once and for all.

If an inhuman entity had inhabited the building, it had finally departed. However, that wouldn't be true of any human entities. They would still be present, unaffected by the cleansing. And even if we managed to convince them to leave, the possibility of bodily remains beneath the building made us wonder if other human spirits wouldn't appear in their place.

For the time being, Kristyn felt better about living there. However, we had a feeling that our work in her town wasn't done. We believed that we would have to return to Reading in the future.

And we were right. But as time went on, Kristyn was less and less put off by the human activity in her building. In fact, she began to embrace it. She asked us a bunch of questions each and every time we spoke with her, because she wanted to know more about it.

Finally, a couple of years after we met her, she asked us the biggest question—if we had room for her in T.A.P.S. By that time, we had gotten to know Kristyn pretty well. We knew that she was a loyal, dedicated, and straightforward person who could get a job done faster and better than most anyone else.

There were times when she might tick people off, but that was because she was on a mission and the mission came first. We also knew that she could be funny as heck, that she laughed straight from her soul, and that she was great company. So naturally we made her a case manager.

After a while, we also gave her the opportunity to teach a course at T.A.P.S. headquarters called Paranormal 101, which was intended to prepare people to conduct their own paranormal investigations. From the beginning, Kristyn was a natural at it. People loved her authoritative but encouraging manner, not to mention her openness about her own experiences.

Of course, Kristyn eventually chose to leave her apartment in Massachusetts for someplace closer to our office in Warwick, and therefore left behind the spirits that were haunting the place. But it seems she's inadvertently taken some of them with her, based on the accounts she has given us.

My guess is we'll be investigating her new place as well before too long.

GHOST HUNTER'S MANUAL: THE OUIJA BOARD

William Fuld wasn't the guy who came up with the idea of the infamous "talking" Ouija board, but he's the one generally credited with its invention. Fuld, who was born in Baltimore, Maryland, was a foreman at the Kennard Novelty Co. when its owner, Charles W. Kennard, was removed from the company—for reasons unknown—in 1891. Kennard Novelty's biggest asset was a talking board patent purchased from a man named Elijah Bond the year before.

The "talking board" was actually composed of two boards,

both of them made of wood. One was a rectangular piece, on which was engraved the alphabet, a series of numbers, and the words "Yes," "No," and "Good-bye." The other board—a flat, heart-shaped piece called a planchette—was supported by two casters and sat directly on the rectangular board.

One person sat down on either side of the planchette. Then both of them placed their fingertips on it as lightly as they could, and asked a question. After a moment, the differential pressure of their fingertips caused the planchette to roam around the rectangular board. Wherever it stopped, the word, letter, or number below it was considered all or part of the answer to their question.

The talking board became a big hit in the late 1800s—and not just among the middle class. It was also seen at the parties of the rich and powerful, who were intrigued by its promise of predicting the future. It also appeared to tap into an undiscovered source of wisdom.

Anyway, Fuld must have done a bang-up job at Kennard, because by 1892 he was named supervisor of the entire company. Immediately, he changed its name to The Ouija Novelty Company, moved it to a new location, and boosted production of Bond's invention, which he dubbed the "Ouija board."

Fuld's exotic name for the board was an attempt to capitalize on the American public's fascination with the mysterious Far East. He let it be known that Ouija was the Egyptian word for "good luck," though there was no absolutely factual basis for this claim. It's more likely that he got the name from the city of Oujda, which is located in the eastern part of Morocco.

Whether it was because of the name "Ouija" or because

of the appeal of the boards themselves, sales of Fuld's product went through the roof. In 1898, Fuld and his brother started their own talking board manufacturing business under the name Isaac Fuld & Brother, leasing the name "Ouija" from The Ouija Novelty Company. It's said that Fuld never took credit for the boards, but in a way he did—because every board carried the name of his company and was clearly stamped with the word "inventor."

With the talking board market booming, Fuld moved in 1919 to introduce the "Mystifying Oracle," a cheaper version of the Ouija board. He also trademarked the names "Egyptian Luck board" and "WE-JA." People who bought talking boards under these names probably didn't know they were all the same basic product, put out by the same company.

Naturally, Fuld encountered fierce competition from other manufacturers. However, he wasn't shy about taking people to court when their companies infringed on his trademarks or patents, a quality that helped him dominate the market and rake in, by his own estimate, upward of a million dollars in profit.

Fuld's death in 1927 was bizarre, as one might expect from the man who had popularized the Ouija board. He climbed up to the roof of his three-story factory, reportedly to make sure a new flagpole was installed properly. However, he should have been as careful about testing the rail he was leaning on, which suddenly gave way and sent him plunging to the ground below.

Some say it wasn't the rail that did him in, but a sudden, overwhelming impulse to fling himself from the roof. Why would such a rich, successful man want to commit suicide?

Even today, no one seems to have an answer to that question—though some say his stock in trade, the mysterious and exotic Ouija board, had something to do with it. In any case, Fuld died of his injuries at the hospital a few hours later, leaving all of his considerable wealth and patents to his heirs.

Decades after Fuld's demise, his family decided to sell his company to Parker Brothers, the toy and game manufacturer that had already made its fortune with products like Monopoly. Parker Brothers, now a part of Hasbro, still owns exclusive rights to the Ouija board and produces them to this day.

So the Ouija board is just a toy, right? Not in our experience here at T.A.P.S. And we're far from alone in this belief.

A great many who believe in the supernatural say the Ouija board is a doorway to another plane of existence. Maybe in some sense it is. People also say that if you're going to use one of these boards, you should place a silver coin on it to keep evil spirits from passing through it into our mortal realm.

This may be an adequate protection, and then again it may not be. The question is . . . do you want to take that chance?

Jason: The Blizzard

2000

The Eshelmann family of Skowhegan, Maine, owned a real gem, a twenty-six-room farmhouse that had been built back in the 1800s. It was a huge, sprawling place, more than big enough for Gary and Diane Eshelmann, their two daughters, their son, and his girlfriend. In fact, they had rooms in the house that they had never even unlocked.

In the two or three lifetimes the house had been standing there, it must have seen a lot of happiness and grief. When the Eshelmanns called us, it was mostly grief. They were having a bad time of it and they didn't know why.

At all hours, but especially at night, they heard footsteps, the sound of children crying, and other noises whose sources they couldn't identify. They had been pushed from behind by forces they couldn't see. Small objects had levitated and struck some members of the family.

On one occasion, Robert—the son—had felt scratching sensations in the areas of his groin and chest. When he checked the affected areas, he discovered long, red scratch marks in his skin. The marks had gone away since then, but his fear of what made them seemed to have remained with him.

Clearly, the family needed help. We hate to refuse people in need, even if it's the middle of the winter and there's bad weather in the forecast. So we packed up our stuff, took along a bigger complement of investigators than usual—eight of us in all—because of the sheer size of the place, and headed for the frozen north.

Also accompanying us was our friend Jodi Picoult, the bestselling author. Jodi had tagged along on a couple of other investigations, and she was eager to see what this one held in store for us. She was also another pair of hands, and in this case we needed all the hands we could get.

One thing we wouldn't have to worry about was a place to stay. With twenty-six rooms, the Eshelmanns could have entertained a crew twice our size and still had beds left over. It's always a plus to be able to stay in the place we're investigating, because then we get a feel for it we can't get otherwise.

Just as the weatherman predicted, we had to contend with the beginnings of a snowstorm as we left Rhode Island. As we made our way up toward the Bay State, the weather got more and more ominous, more and more difficult to drive through. By the time we reached the Maine border, we were fighting a full-blown blizzard.

A group with more brains would have turned back, no question about it. We kept going, all the way up to Skowhegan. And somehow we found the farmhouse we were looking for, though we could barely see the road in front of us.

The Eshelmanns were great people, who couldn't believe we had kept our appointment in such a blinding snowstorm. Of course, getting there was only half the battle. The other half was keeping the snow out of our equipment as we unpacked it.

Keith Johnson, Ed Baines, and I interviewed the family while Grant and the others conducted a walkthrough of the house. The Eshelmanns were relieved to have us there. They couldn't wait to find out the reason for all the activity in their home.

Right from the beginning, we began to get a sense of what the family had been going through. Doors slammed in our faces, without any rational explanation. A couple of our investigators felt something hot against their skin and, moments later, found scratches there. There was growling coming from somewhere in the house, though we couldn't figure out where.

We experienced one temperature change after another, all throughout the house. First we would record sixty-eight degrees, then it would rise to ninety degrees, and afterward it would plummet to forty degrees. The changes were drastic, and therefore unlikely to have natural causes.

More than once, we smelled something foul in the house. Before we could identify the source of the odor, it was gone, even though the windows were closed tightly and there wasn't any breeze around to dispel it. Then, a few minutes later, we smelled it again in a different part of the house.

These were bad smells, the worst kind of garbage smells, like pure sulfur, like rotten eggs. The kind of smells you couldn't tolerate no matter how hard you tried. They stuck to your clothes and stayed with you.

We also found ourselves plagued by energy surges, our EMF meters jumping all over the place. There was no natural explanation for the activity, as far as we could tell. We logged the data and continued our investigation.

At one point that first night, our friend Jodi told us that she felt a presence in the room. By then, we were feeling the same thing. I can only describe it as a heaviness in the air, a sense that there was something unhealthy in the vicinity.

Normally, we don't get too excited about globules. However, we saw more than our share this time. They just gave us more evidence to work with, more support for the conclusions at which we would ultimately arrive.

The most dramatic activity came on the second night of the investigation. As Grant and I were walking through the den, we felt something hit us. Looking down at the floor, we saw a couple of remote controls lying at our feet. We were sure they hadn't been there the last time we passed through the room.

Hearing noises in the barn, we went to check them out. However, we couldn't find anything. As we were about to leave, we saw something shoot across the barn. And not just one something—several of them. They had weight to them, too, judging by the way they crashed against the walls.

They turned out to be wooden boards. We didn't know if whatever threw them had intended to hit us with them. But if they *had* hit us, they would definitely have done some damage.

Later, as Grant and I were going from bedroom to bedroom, a dark figure appeared in front of us. It was roughly the size of a man, and it didn't seem daunted by us in the least. Only when we got close enough to touch it did it fade away, leaving us standing by ourselves in the hallway.

Sometimes we come up with little or nothing in the way of data, even when we've had significant experiences in a place. In this case there was plenty of data as well. As we listened to the hours of tape we had recorded, we heard some of the most distinct EVPs we've ever come across.

One said, "Get out." Another said, "Come to hell." Not "*Go* to hell," as one of the living might say. It sounded as if whoever—or *what*ever—had used the words was already there.

We had seen and heard enough by this time to be certain that the house was haunted, and not by a gentle spirit. Judging by the violence it had used against us, we were dealing with a negative entity, and therefore a dangerous one. We didn't want to leave the Eshelmanns at its mercy, and since we had brought Keith with us, we suggested a ritual cleansing of the house.

They agreed, and Keith got started. Going from room to room, Keith recited the blessings he had brought with him, methodically cutting off the entity from one part of the house after another. It was important to have a plan, because without one the entity could find a place to hole up and reassert itself at a later date.

In conducting our investigation, we hadn't found it necessary to enter all twenty-six rooms in the house. But we had to do so now. Keith had his work cut out for him as never before. After all, cleansing a place isn't just a matter of saying words out of a book. There's a struggle involved, and it can wear a man out—even when he's dealing with just six or seven rooms.

Finally, we came to the end of the line. We had just two more spaces to deal with—the attic and the kitchen. There was just one problem. We couldn't get up into the attic because, since we were dealing with an old farmhouse, the supports weren't made to hold a person's weight.

There was only one way to reach the Eshelmanns' attic, and that was through a small window on the side of the house. Unfortunately, it was pretty high up. To make use of it, someone would have to climb up the side of the house. In good weather, it wouldn't have been such a big deal. In a raging blizzard . . . that was another story.

And even if we accessed the window, we could only sprinkle holy water on the near end. The rest of the attic would go without, and therefore continue to serve as a safe harbor for the negative entity. Unless, of course, we found a way to shoot the holy water across the attic to the other side.

"We need a super soaker," said Grant, who was known to come up with a good idea now and then.

"We've got one," said Gary Eshelmann. "I mean, if you're serious."

"We are," I assured him.

But we still had to get up to the attic window to shoot in the holy water. The Eshelmanns had a ladder we could use, which could be extended to the necessary height. But the way it was snowing, it would be a treacherous ascent, to say the least.

"I'd have to be crazy to even think about it," I said, shading my eyes from falling snowflakes to eyeball the attic window.

A few minutes later, I was climbing the Eshelmanns' aluminum ladder in a world of swirling, driving snow, a kid's super soaker full of holy water in one hand and a rung of the ladder in the other. The bottoms of my boots were caked with snow and ice, so it was slippery going. But somehow, I made it to the top.

"Here goes," I yelled down.

Then I shot a stream of water across the attic. At the same time, I could hear Keith on the ground below, speaking his blessings into the wind. His voice sounded far away, muted by the falling snow.

Another shot of water. Another blessing. Another shot. Another blessing. And so on. I'm sure Keith could have kept going for a good long time, he had so many blessings stored in his head. But the super soaker was out of water.

"That's it," I said. "I'm coming down."

First, I tossed down the super soaker. Then I started to descend. By then, my knees were stiff and my hands were kind of frozen, so it was difficult to negotiate the rungs of the ladder. But I wasn't going to let myself fall. After all, Grant would never let me hear the end of it.

Finally, I reached the bottom rung, which was all but buried in snow. Letting my other foot dangle, I searched for the ground—and found it. A moment later, I was back on terra firma. Grant and a couple of our teammates lowered the ladder.

"Did you get all of it?" Keith asked me, wondering how much of the attic I had reached with the holy water.

"I certainly hope so," was the best answer I could give him. "I sure as heck don't want to go back up there."

Of course, even if I'd been successful in the attic, we weren't finished. We still had to bless the kitchen. But that would be a whole lot warmer and a whole lot less precarious than the work I had just done.

"Hey," someone said, "where's the ladder?"

I looked around. We had just taken it down from the side of the house a couple of minutes earlier. And yet, as deep as the snow was and as quickly as it was coming down, we couldn't see the ladder anymore.

Fortunately, the Eshelmanns didn't take us to task for losing it. And of course, it wasn't really lost. They wound up finding it on the ground a couple of months later when they had their spring thaw. But at the time, it was a pretty bizarre experience. We had lost cables, thermoses, batteries, and even a couple of pieces of equipment in the course of one investigation or another, but never an entire ladder.

Anyway, we made the kitchen our next stop. After we took our boots off and warmed up a bit, Keith started the final phase of the cleansing. Each blessing he spoke got a reaction in the form of a growl, as if a wild animal had snuck into the house and was trying to scare us out of it.

Finally, the growling stopped. Scattered around the Eshelmanns' kitchen, we looked at each other hopefully. But there was one last thing that had to take place before we knew the cleansing had been effective.

"Can you give us a sign of your departure?" Keith asked.

For a moment, nothing happened. Then the birdcage behind me rattled as if it were going to shake itself apart. Only for a couple of seconds, of course, though it seemed like much longer. After that the kitchen was still again.

As far as any of us could tell, the entity was gone. It wasn't the easiest investigation we had ever embarked on, that was for sure. Between the size of the farmhouse and the adverse weather conditions, we had undertaken quite a task. But we had gotten it done, and that was satisfying for everyone concerned.

We still see the Eshelmanns now and then. They say they haven't had any trouble in their twenty-six-room farmhouse since we left. Which is a good thing, because I'm not too eager to get back up on that ladder.

GHOST HUNTER'S MANUAL: POLTERGEISTS

Poltergeist is a German word that means "noisy spirit." However, there have been reports of poltergeists in a great many places around the world. The oldest of them date all the way back to ancient Rome, and accounts of the Roman army being assaulted by a swarm of flying stones.

Poltergeist activity usually starts off innocently. You hear a few knocks and bangs that could be the result of a branch falling on the roof or a door swinging in the wind. But when you check around the house, you can't find an explanation.

The next thing that happens is the furniture starts moving. At first, you're not sure it happened. After all, none of us expects to find a chair or a couch in a different place or position, especially if it's been sitting there for a long time. But it happens, and we're left scratching our heads as to why.

Then the situation starts to heat up. You hear voices, and not the friendly kind. You may even see a ghostly figure staring at you from a doorway. Shutters rattle. The furniture starts to slide across the room, right in front of your eyes. Beds shake, sometimes violently. Dishes go flying and shatter at your feet.

Poltergeist activity can last for just a few seconds or go on for much longer. There have been reports of spirits making their presence felt only on a single night, never to return. But there are also cases of such activity lasting for years, slowly gaining in intensity over time.

No two poltergeist situations are the same. However, while several people may witness the actions of the poltergeist, it usually has an affinity for a particular member of the household. In fact, there may be little or no activity unless that individual is present, and the activity may stop when that person leaves the premises.

This member of the household may be especially stressed out at the time of the poltergeist incidents. He or she may be dealing with some extreme, negative emotions. If this is the case, see that the individual involved gets some medical care, and soon afterward the activity is likely to subside.

Quite often, poltergeist activity is linked to an adolescent female. Girls are going through all sorts of changes as they approach adolescence, and anyone who has had a daughter that age knows how volatile they can be. Poltergeists are drawn to that volatility like a piranha to fresh meat.

Sometimes poltergeist activity is the work of several spirits rather than just one. After all, a single spirit can only do so much to draw attention to itself. Working together and pooling their energy, a group of spirits can be strong enough to move large objects and make loud noises.

Ultimately, a poltergeist is like any other spirit. In order to rid yourself of it, you just need to determine the root of its anger, maybe with the help of a clairvoyant. Then you can help it pass over.

Of course, you may never know the reason for a spirit's unrest. But then, a lot of people who have experienced a poltergeist don't *want* to know why it showed up. They're just happy to see it go.

Probably the best-known and the most enduring poltergeist haunting on record occurred at a place called Borley Rectory, in Essex, England. The rectory, a large brick building, was raised in 1863 beside the old, twelfth-century Borley Church by the Reverend Henry Dawson Ellis Bull, who demolished an older house to make way for the new one. It burned to the ground seventy-six years later, but not before spawning all kinds of mysterious reports.

The first came from a man named Jeffrey Shaw. In 1885, he claimed that he had seen stones flying through the air in the vicinity of the rectory—not thrown by a human being, but flying *on their own*. Unfortunately, there's no documentation describing the parish's reaction at the time, so we don't know if Shaw was taken seriously.

However, later that same year, a nun was seen by the

headmaster of the grammar school walking on the grounds of the rectory. It wasn't anyone with whom the headmaster was familiar, and her expression suggested that she was lost. When he pursued her to see if he could assist her in finding her way, she seemed to disappear into thin air.

It wasn't the last time the headmaster would catch sight of the nun. In fact, throughout that year and the next, she seemed to turn up all the time, always with the same blank expression on her face. Yet, try as he might, he could never catch up to her.

In 1886, a woman by the name of Mrs. E. Byford was working in the rectory when she heard the sound of footsteps in the next room. When she went to investigate, she couldn't find the person responsible. It wouldn't have been all that alarming an experience if she hadn't heard the footsteps again and again, day after day, not to mention other noises she couldn't account for. Mrs. Byford wound up quitting her job at the rectory, certain that the place was haunted.

The Reverend Henry Bull died on May 7, 1892, after having fathered fourteen children, for whom he had to expand the structure of the rectory. One of his sons, who was also named Henry Bull, eventually came to serve as rector of Borley. Like his father, he heard and saw a great many strange things at the rectory, none of which was ever explained to anyone's satisfaction.

On June 9, 1927, the younger Henry Bull died. The rectory remained empty for more than a year after his death. Then, in early October, the Reverend Guy Eric Smith and his wife optimistically took up residence there. It wasn't long, however, before the property began to live up to its reputation. Smith's wife, who had a mind to clean out the long-unused kitchen, found a paper bag inside a cupboard. When she opened it, she saw that it contained a human skull.

Though the Smiths moved into the rectory with hopes of living a normal life, it was anything but normal there. They often heard the ringing of servant bells, though the strings to the bells had been cut before they arrived. They also heard footsteps and saw lights moving outside the house.

The last straw was when Mrs. Smith caught sight of a horse-drawn carriage one night, its black bulk gliding along the road that led up to the rectory. When she went outside to see who was visiting at such a late hour, the carriage vanished before her eyes. Neither she nor her husband could take any more. Less than two years after they arrived, the Smiths packed their things and moved out.

It took the parish a while to find a replacement. No one was at all surprised. In fact, with everything that had happened to the rectory's previous occupants, it looked as if the house might remain vacant for good.

At last, the Reverend Lionel Foyster and his family agreed to move in. Foyster, a first cousin of the Bulls, had to have known what he was getting himself into. Nonetheless, he, his wife, Marianne, and their adopted daughter, Adelaide, made the rectory their home in October 1930.

Right from the beginning, the family was confronted with the same assortment of bizarre phenomena that had plagued Borley's previous residents. Marianne Foyster said that she had seen papers appear out of nowhere. Strange, scrawled writings showed up on the walls, then faded again before she could decipher them. A terrified Adelaide informed her parents that she had been attacked by something in the house, though she couldn't say what it was.

Lionel Foyster had some strange experiences of his own. He reported a ghostly appearance by the late Henry Bull on one occasion, and things flying out the door on another. Glass objects materialized out of thin air, bells rang day and night, and windows were smashed. Lionel was alarmed, to say the least.

An exorcism was performed at the Foysters' request, but it didn't seem to have any effect. Shortly after the ceremony, Marianne was attacked—not just once, but several times. The assaults always seemed to come when she was alone. At one point she was thrown out of her bed by something she couldn't see.

Still, the Foysters remained in the house as long as they could. Finally, after they had put up with seven years' worth of daily torment, Lionel became ill and the family lost its will to stay at the rectory. In May 1937, they at last allowed whatever was haunting the place to drive them out.

In the period from 1930 through 1935 alone, more than two thousand poltergeist events were reported in and about the rectory. In some cases, people saw moving objects or apparitions. In others, they only heard noises. And the reports didn't end when the rectory was destroyed by fire in 1939. Neighbors continued to catch glimpses of ghostly coaches and lonely female figures dressed in nun's clothing.

A number of old tales have been dug up in attempts to explain the activity at the rectory. One of them tells of a monk from the Benedictine monastery in the vicinity of Borley Church, who eloped with a young nun from the nearby Bures Nunnery. Eventually the lovers were caught and the monk was hanged for his indiscretion. But according to the tales, the nun suffered an even worse fate—she was buried alive in a stone wall of the nunnery, and left to wither away.

Was this the nun seen by the headmaster of the grammar school back in the 1880s, desperately seeking burial in holy ground? Were the scrabbled writings seen on the wall back in the 1930s her attempts to communicate with the living? Was she responsible for the ghostly footsteps, ringing bells, and flying stones that were experienced at Borley over the years?

What do *you* think?

Grant: There Was an Old Woman . . .

2000

An elderly woman. Looking out at us from the window." Sheila Sullivan shivered a little, her skin pale, her green eyes screwed up tight. Clearly, she was frightened out of her wits. "And I've seen her on the stairs, too. Looking right back at me."

Her husband, John, nodded, his expression long and grim. "I've seen her as well. Sometimes she's in our room. I wake up and I see her leaving, moving out into the hall. When I get up to follow, she's gone."

Their son, Sean, who was fourteen, didn't seem quite as scared as his parents, though he noted that he had heard laughter in the house, even when he was alone. Also, banging sounds in the walls and a scratching coming from the attic. His parents had heard the same sounds, both when they were together and when they were alone.

We had arrived at the Sullivans' two-bedroom, saltbox colonial in southwest Massachusetts earlier that afternoon. But it had been days since the family first made contact with T.A.P.S. through our website. Right from the start, it was evident to us that they were unequipped to cope with the intensity of their experiences.

While Jason and I were interviewing the family, our team was setting up equipment throughout their home. Cole Morris and Ed Gaines, who had accompanied us to the Sullivan residence, were as cheerful and efficient as ever. Obviously, they felt perfectly comfortable in the house—a great deal more so than its owners.

Were the Sullivans just easily spooked? Or was there something going on in their house that was driving them to the brink? That was what we had come to find out.

We placed two of our cameras at the end of a long hallway, one of them facing the bathroom and the other facing back toward the dining room and the rest of the house. We made sure that the living room fireplace was in view of the second camera, as some activity had been reported there.

Then we waited.

The first significant sign came at about one o'clock in the morning, when Sheila drew our attention to some knocking sounds. They weren't very loud, but she had heard them so often that she knew what to listen for. Jason and I responded by taking a look around the house.

We were plumbers, so the first thing we looked at was the plumbing. We determined that the sounds were coming from pipes in the walls, which were cooling for the night. Nothing ghostly so far.

Sean, who couldn't sleep with our investigation going

on, was camped out in front of the fireplace when Jason and I returned to the living room. There was a glass of water sitting on the floor beside him, which he had brought in while we were gone. As we discussed the pipe situation with the Sullivans, an ember popped out of the fireplace and landed on the back of Sean's hand.

Anyone who's ever had a fireplace knows that embers shoot out sometimes, propelled by expanding gases in the wood. Usually, these embers cool off before they have a chance to do any harm. However, this one had landed right on the boy's skin, and it was big enough to have burned him.

Fortunately, it never had the chance. His glass of water tipped over, spilled on his hand, and doused the ember. Just like that, without anyone touching it.

Neither John nor Cole had seen the glass move, but the rest of us had. As we considered the implications, Jason pointed to the steps and said, "Over there!" Whirling, I caught a glimpse of a woman rounding the top of the stairs.

Jason was the first one up the stairs, but I was right behind him. We searched the upstairs rooms, but couldn't find anyone. Jason look frustrated. Whoever or whatever we had seen had vanished on us.

By then, Cole and Ed had joined us upstairs. Just as we were about to rejoin the Sullivans in the living room, we heard a faint sound. Signaling for quiet, I listened as intently as I could.

Jason turned to me and mouthed a word: *singing*. I nodded. Because that's what it sounded like—a woman's voice, singing something soft and gentle.

After a few moments, it stopped. But it was replaced by

another sound. A scratching, coming from above us. Ed volunteered to check out the attic. Armed with a flashlight, he made his way upstairs.

We gave him some time to look around. Then I asked, "Do you see anything?"

"I do," he said.

"What is it?" asked Jason.

Ed chuckled. "Mice."

Some time later, as Jason and I were sitting in the living room, we caught sight of a swarm of globules ascending the stairs. Again we bolted out of our seats, this time hoping to get a sense of where the globules were headed. But by the time we reached the stairs, they were gone.

The rest of the night was uneventful, but we had more than enough to chew on. We had seen the glass tip over and douse the ember on Sean's hand. We had glimpsed the figure of a woman at the top of the stairs. We had heard the singing and we had seen the globules. When we left the Sullivans in the early morning, we told them we believed there was paranormal activity in the house.

Still, we wanted to check out our audio and video recordings. It's nice when you have two or more members of the team eyeballing the same phenomenon, but not as good as when you have hard evidence.

Back at Jason's house in Rhode Island, we went over the hours and hours of data we had collected. For a long time, nothing popped out at us. Then we caught the sound of a woman singing in one of the audio recordings, just about the time we had seen the woman and bolted up the stairs.

That felt good. It corroborated our experiences in the house. But as it turned out, we were going to get even more corroboration. A stretch of video recording revealed the globules we had seen near the stairs, each one bright and round and fairly distinct.

So we had two pieces of evidence supporting the Sullivans' claims of supernatural activity, which was enough for us to say with confidence that their house was haunted. Most likely it was a single spirit, that of an old woman. However, our research uncovered nothing unusual in the history of the place, so that was all we could say.

The next move was the Sullivans'. Before our investigation, they would have wanted us to get rid of the spirit, no matter what it took. But after seeing how it saved Sean from harm and hearing the recording of its singing, which was quite pleasant, they had a change of heart.

We've followed up with the family over the years. In that time, they've grown quite attached to their supernatural house guest, and can't believe they ever found anything frightening about her.

GHOST HUNTER'S MANUAL: ADVANCE RESEARCH

There's no debate among paranormal investigators that research is part of the job. For some of us, who like nothing better than rolling up our sleeves and delving into dusty old books and microfiche, it may be the best part of the job. The question, when it comes to research, isn't whether to do it. It's *when*.

If you're simply hunkering down in an old graveyard with your camera and a recording device, looking for ghostly images and EVPs, you need to do some research in advance. Otherwise, you won't know where to go or when to do so. But if you are involved in a full-fledged investigation, in which clients are depending on you for help, you need to do your research after the fact.

People always ask us why we don't research a place *before* we embark on an investigation. The reason is that we try to be as scientific as possible. If we have preconceived notions about a place, it will skew the way we approach it—not to mention our experiences there.

When you visit a venue, whether it's a house or anything else, you want to start off with a clean slate. You don't want to let the stories about the place poke holes in your objectivity. For instance, if you read that a little girl was killed in the home a hundred years earlier, you'll have that little girl in the back of your mind as you proceed with your investigation. Every time something happens, whether it's a knocking sound or the appearance of a suspicious shadow, you'll be tempted to say it's caused by the spirit of the little girl.

You may even overlook legitimate paranormal events because your mind is focused elsewhere. For example, if you know a man died in a certain closet you'll probably concentrate your investigation on that closet and be less vigilant when it comes to the rest of the home. But if your efforts are untainted by prior knowledge, you may find that another room is *way* more active than the closet you read about.

Rather than learning too much about a place beforehand,

log every event and observation in the course of your investigation for later study. Be as thorough as possible. Then, after you've collected your data, you can research the history of the venue and compare your notes with whatever you find.

Not only has your data-gathering been free of undue influences, but you also get the satisfaction of seeing your observations and theories line up with established fact. This is a good way to measure your capabilities as an investigator. If what you've found aligns with your research, you're on the right track.

Clearly, it's better to embark on an investigation with an open mind. However, there is one bit of research you may want to do before arriving at a client's home. You may want to know something about that person, without prying too much. Then you can more reliably determine if the problem is what's taking place in the person's home or what's taking place in his or her head.

Though most clients are accurately reporting what they've experienced, often at the cost of great trauma, some are just plagued by overactive imaginations. Still others, as we've learned from experience, are making it all up to serve their own agendas—like the guy who told us he had a ghost in the wall when all he wanted to do was get on TV. If possible, it's good to have an inkling of the client's reputation going in. You may not decide to decline an investigation because of it, but it's good to have all your information in front of you.

Jason: In Thrall

2000

Bill and Dani Turner said they had never dabbled in the occult, nor did they know anyone who had done so. Nevertheless, something had been invited into their house that was more than they could deal with.

On more than one occasion, Dani had seen a white-haired man in 1920s-style clothing walking through the house. When she finally got up the nerve to confront him, he disappeared. But he wasn't gone for good. He appeared again, just as regularly as before their confrontation.

The children were affected as well. One time, when they were playing video games in the living room, they felt something pull their controllers out of their hands. The next thing they knew, the controllers were flying across the room.

There were also instances in which various members of the family had been shoved from behind. At first, they thought it was each other. Then they started to suspect something more sinister.

Frightened, they called in T.A.P.S. When we arrived—along with a Catholic priest named Kevin—we assured the family that we would do everything we could to get to the root of their problem. If it was of a paranormal nature, we would let them know it. And if it wasn't, we would let them know that as well.

In accordance with our regular procedures, we took a walk through the house, with a particular emphasis on the living room and the bedrooms. We did this partly to determine the best locations for our cameras and audio recorders, but we also wanted to see what the family might have been up to.

If we find movies or books about the occult, we get some idea of how the paranormal may have gotten a foothold in the house—if indeed that's what happened. If we find a Ouija board, we get even more insight into the problem. But in this case, we found none of those things. The Turners' interests seemed to run more toward romantic comedies than the supernatural.

We did find something else, however. A short time after Grant and I split up to cover the house more efficiently, he called me from down the hall. Following his voice, I joined him in a storage area—actually, little more than a crawl space.

"Take a look at this," he said.

The walls were covered with occult symbols and names. Among them were several references to Astaroth, a well-known demonic entity. Obviously, these drawings were at the root of the problems in the house.

"We need to confront them with this," I said.

Grant nodded. "Without a doubt."

The Turners were adamant that they weren't responsible for what we had found in the storage area. In fact, though they were aware of the drawings, they hadn't ever looked at them closely enough to know what they were. We believed them. It was likely the previous owners of the home who had created the drawings, an outgrowth of some level of involvement in the occult.

Later that night, we caught a glimpse of a human-looking figure—but just a glimpse. When we tried to take a closer look, there was no one there. Had we encountered the old man the Turners had mentioned? We couldn't tell.

We also heard growling coming from the bedrooms. When we checked them out, we failed to find anything that could have made such sounds. But we heard them again and again as the night went on.

Grant and I called the investigation at about four-thirty in the morning. Advising the family that we would review our data and get back to them, we packed up our vehicle and went back to Warwick. Then we began the laborious process of going over several hours of recordings.

We heard the growling on one of the tapes, which backed up what we had experienced at the house. In addition, we caught a single EVP. It said, "Please help me."

The next day, we paid Bill and Dani a visit and sat down with them in their living room. They already knew part of what we were going to say. After all, we had discussed with them the occult drawings we had discovered in their storage area, and told them that such symbols were an invitation to demonic entities. However, they were surprised when they got the rest of the story.

"Actually, there are two entities here," I told them. "One is human, the other one inhuman. And the human one is under the control of the inhuman one."

It was the only conclusion that made sense. The figure of the old man that the family had seen was the human spirit, maybe a previous resident of the house, doing its best to communicate with them. Had it been on its own, it would only have engaged in mild attention-getting behavior.

But the Turners had been shoved from behind and had objects ripped from their hands. That wasn't typical behavior for a human spirit. That was the work of something a lot more violent, a lot more malicious—an inhuman entity trying to frighten them into leaving their house.

"Is there anything we can do about it?" Dani asked.

We suggested that Kevin be allowed to cleanse the place. It was the only way, we said, to get rid of the demonic entity that was plaguing them. Then we could worry about the human entity, if it was still a problem once the demon was gone. The Turners were happy to accept our recommendation.

Kevin proceeded with the ritual. At first it was very quiet, the only sound that of his voice. Then the inhuman entity in the house reacted to Kevin's religious provocation—with a vengeance.

In the kitchen, cabinet doors started to open and close. Growling noises came from everywhere at once. There were thin, high-pitched screams and foul odors, and the air around us got fifteen degrees warmer.

Suddenly, it all stopped. Kevin had finished his blessing. From every indication, the inhuman entity was gone.

We checked back with the Turners weeks later. They had painted over the occult words and symbols in their storage room and hadn't seen any further signs of paranormal activity, including evidence of the old man. Their ordeal was over.

GHOST HUNTER'S MANUAL: HUMAN VERSUS INHUMAN

Over the years, we have come across other instances in which an inhuman entity is controlling a human one, just like the situation we found at the Turners'. There are certain signs we have learned to look for, certain indications that this type of thing is going on.

As we note elsewhere in this book, human entities don't often hurt people—not of their own accord. They become visible from time to time, make noises, and engage in other attention-getting behavior. Sometimes, they go so far as to slam a door in someone's face. But that's really the extent of it.

A demonic entity, on the other hand, can be as vicious as a wounded wolverine. If it can hurt people, great. If it can drive them out of their house, even better. It has no regard whatsoever for anyone living or dead.

Which is why you can tell, sometimes, that the human spirit under the demon's control isn't happy about the arrangement. The human entity may look sad or oppressed. It may be missing its hands, its feet, or one of its eyes.

In some cases, the inhuman entity goes so far as to impersonate the human one, all with the intention of doing mischief to its living victims. It may appear in the guise of the human entity, beg for someone to follow it, and then push its unsuspecting victim down a flight of stairs. Or it may lure someone into a room, lead him to a particular wall, and then shove a bookcase over on him.

Generally, there are ways to tell when a demonic entity is impersonating the human variety. If you listen to the spirit's pleas, they have a sinister edge to them. Or the spirit's appearance is accompanied by an odd or displeasing smell.

The point is that you can't let your guard down. Even if you're certain you're dealing with a human spirit, you have to exercise care. You may have a more serious problem on your hands than you think.

Grant: Molested

2000

We weren't the first paranormal investigators to visit Sharon Wallace at her house in central Connecticut. Another group had looked over her house a couple of weeks earlier and told her it was being haunted by an incubus, which is a malevolent supernatural entity that lies on top of women for the purpose of having intercourse with them.

If that group was right, it explained why Sharon was having nightmares about feeling the touch of hands on her body, and why she felt that she was being penetrated by something electrically stimulating. Sometimes, she claimed, she could still feel the penetration as she woke up. At other times, she could see a dark figure exiting the room, but couldn't make out any of its features.

Sharon's husband, Bill, didn't know what to think.

Sharon also said she felt hot and cold spots throughout their house, but he didn't feel any such thing. Normally he would have been skeptical about the possibility of his house being haunted by a demon, but his wife's discomfort made him think twice.

Confused and concerned, he had accepted the concept of the incubus, and said that he wanted the entity out of his house. Apparently, the other group had performed a rite of exorcism, but it hadn't produced any positive results. He was hoping that our group would do a better job.

Jason and I sat down and talked to Sharon and Bill, a couple in their early fifties, while our colleagues Ed and Brittney started looking for places to set up our equipment. We explained to the Wallaces that we couldn't go by the findings of another ghost-hunting outfit, which might have drawn conclusions without any real evidence. We felt we had to conduct our own investigation, using scientific equipment and following scientific procedures, before we pronounced a place haunted.

The Wallaces understood. After all, the other group hadn't managed to improve the situation for Sharon. The couple trusted us and our approach, and said they would do anything necessary to cooperate with our investigation.

Clearly, Sharon was beside herself. The idea that a malevolent entity was sexually assaulting her had been preying on her mind, making her absolutely miserable. We could see that she hadn't slept well in a while.

As always, our team set up equipment in all the key locations. In this case, that meant cameras and audio devices in the master bedroom, where Sharon had experienced many of the violations she described, as well as in the upstairs bathroom and a couple of the other rooms where she had felt hot or cold spots.

By about eight-thirty, we were set to hunker down and see what we could find. A couple of hours later, we still hadn't seen or heard any sign of an entity, but that didn't mean much. We continued to wait, talk with the Wallaces, and wait some more.

At times Sharon complained that she was burning up, even though there was nothing unusual about the temperature in the house, nor were there any energy fluctuations registering on our EMF meters. We could see the beads of sweat on her face, so we knew she was telling the truth. But whatever was going on, it was affecting her and her alone.

Midnight came and went, and we still hadn't seen a sign of paranormal activity. But it wasn't the lack of evidence that bothered me. It was the feeling I got from the house. Usually, if there's activity in a place, I can sense it. In this case, I wasn't sensing anything at all.

Not that we were going to give up. Neither Jason nor I had proven infallible when it comes to these feelings. That's why we used equipment like video cameras, EMF meters, and audio recorders—because feelings aren't foolproof.

The group that visited the Wallaces before us relied on feelings alone, and they came to the conclusion that the house was haunted. But the longer I sat there, the more I wondered if there was any truth to their findings.

Later on, Jason told me that he wasn't feeling anything either. We stuck it out the rest of the night, but only because we felt a responsibility to the Wallaces, not because we really expected to find anything. In the end, the night was uneventful, and the only thing we could do was go home and go over what we had recorded.

Sometimes we don't think we've discovered anything, but our tapes prove us wrong. This wasn't one of those times. As carefully as we went over our audio and video recordings, we couldn't find a thing.

We called the Wallaces to let them know the results of our investigation. They were relieved in a way, but puzzled and frustrated in another. After all, they thought they had determined the cause of Sharon's troubles, scary as it might be. Now they were all the way back to square one.

When we investigate a problem, our work doesn't start and end with what you would call ghost-hunting. On occasion we come across a plumbing problem, and if we can we take care of it on the spot. Or we see something that a carpenter or a roofer or an electrician can take care of, and we make that recommendation.

That's because we're there to help, regardless of what form that help might take. Our goal isn't to find a supernatural entity. It's to relieve our clients of whatever is making their lives a living hell.

With that philosophy in mind, we made a list of what Sharon was experiencing and researched the symptoms. It took a while, but we finally found a medical problem that seemed to provide an explanation.

"It's called perimenopause," we explained to Sharon over the phone. "It's a transitional period that takes place before actual menopause, sometimes in women as young as their late thirties. And among their symptoms are sleep disruptions, hot and cold flashes, and emotional distress."

We're not doctors, so we recommended that Sharon find one and see what he had to say. When she did, he confirmed our suspicions. Sharon didn't need an exorcism. All she needed was some kind of hormone therapy.

Once she started her medical treatments, her experiences stopped—including her feelings of penetration, which might simply have been a product of her imagination. As far as we know, she hasn't complained about them since.

GHOST HUNTER'S MANUAL: INCUBUS

According to ancient lore, an incubus is a male demon whose objective is to have sexual intercourse with human beings, usually females. Its name comes from the Latin word *incubo*, which translates into "I lie on top," because it lies on people who are asleep, causing them to feel as if there is a heavy weight on top of them.

Like any inhuman entity, an incubus would require energy in order to sustain itself in our world for any length of time. An incubus could draw that energy from its victim as it sits on top of him or her. So sometimes it wouldn't be just sex that motivates the demon, but also a basic need for sustenance.

One of the earliest references to an incubus was made almost five thousand years ago in Mesopotamia, which is now called Iraq. A text known as the Sumerian King List mentions Lilu, the father of the ancient hero Gilgamesh, as a supernatural entity that seduced women in their sleep. Incubi were also the subject of Christian writings from at least the time of the Middle Ages.

Some stories describe an incubus inhabiting the body of a man or woman. In those cases, they have to be exorcised by priests. In our experience, that's the only way to get rid of an incubus—through religious provocation.

One of the things that makes it difficult to prove the existence of an incubus is that there's a condition called sleep paralysis that has pretty much the same effect on people. As they wake up, they feel that there's a crushing weight on top of them. Their muscles feel paralyzed, they lose control of certain reflexes, and they may have difficulty simply blinking or breathing.

Actually, we all experience sleep paralysis. It takes hold of us when we're deep in sleep. If it didn't, we might flail around in reaction to what's happening in our dreams and hurt ourselves.

Sleep paralysis may last anywhere from a few seconds to several minutes, though to the sleeper it has to seem a lot longer than that. Sometimes it's accompanied by something called hypnopompic hallucinations, which occur naturally in the brain but may be extremely frightening because they may lead the sleeper to think there's a spirit present when there isn't any.

It's up to the ghost hunter to determine if his client is being visited by an inhuman entity or simply suffering from sleep paralysis. He can sometimes make that judgment based on what else is going on in the home. If he's lucky, he'll witness such phenomena as dark masses moving through the house or record EVPs. However, there are times when it's almost impossible to tell the difference between a case of chronic sleep paralysis and a prolonged demonic assault.

Our recommendation, in that case, is to err on the side of caution. Call in someone who's experienced in religious provocation and ask him to cleanse the home. That way, if there *is* an inhuman entity present, the problem will be resolved.

Jason: Beside Herself

2001

Deborah Clendennon had become a forgetful woman. At least, that's what her husband, George, thought.

He would tell her all kinds of things in the course of a day—for instance, that their minivan was due for an inspection, or that their neighbor had won a couple hundred dollars in the state lottery, or that her sister had called while she was out. But to George's dismay, Deborah would forget half of what he told her, claiming that he had never mentioned the minivan or their neighbor or her sister's call.

Just to make sure he wasn't going nuts, George would write down most everything he said after he said it. He would write down the day and the time and everything. And still, a good part of the time his wife would deny his ever mentioning it.

At first, it was just an inconvenience. Then, like anyone in his position, George started to get worried. He didn't know much about split personality disorders, but it seemed to him that his wife might be the victim of one. One time he even mentioned it might be good for her to see a psychologist. The idea didn't sit too well with her. In fact, she balked like crazy—no pun intended—categorically refusing to even consider the idea.

But if Deborah was suffering from a split personality, it might get worse. The Clendennons were only in their late thirties. What might happen to Deborah in the next ten years? The next twenty? Clearly, George had to do something.

As he was trying to figure out *what*, he started seeing a figure in the house—a female that he might have said was his wife, except he only managed to catch glimpses of her out of the corner of his eye. The first time he saw her, he was relaxing in his favorite chair in the living room. The next time he was standing in the kitchen, making himself a sandwich.

Both times George addressed the female, she didn't answer. When he went to track her down, to find out what was wrong, he couldn't find any sign of her. The same type of thing happened over and over again. One time he followed her into a room with no means of egress, and still she managed to vanish somehow.

George began to wonder if his wife's memory lapses and the presence of the female figure might be related. If so, it might not be a psychologist he needed. It might be an expert in paranormal phenomena, though he had never before put much stock in the possibility of the supernatural.

We didn't know what to make of this tendril of light crossing a room in New Hampshire. Was it evidence of something super-natural?

It wasn't a fluke, because we caught it again later on. Could it have been an entity attempting to communicate with us?

You might think this human-looking shadow we caught on a window frame in New Hampshire was cast by one of our investigators, but we take great pains to make sure that sort of thing doesn't happen.

Sizing up the investigations ahead.

If you look closely, you can see a ghostly image in this basement.

Jason gives Grant a leg up.

This dark shape was sprawled across the bed as if it owned the place. Maybe at one time it did.

Our camera caught something out there beyond the door. Is it a spirit or a trick of the light?

We've looked down a lot of lonely hallways, but we never know what we'll find at the end of them.

In this case, what we found looked like an eerie ball of lightning, but was more likely just an orb created by dust.

See that shadow huddled in the corner of the room? Imagine what it felt like to see it in person.

Those ominous-looking clouds over the Spalding Inn are nothing compared to what we found inside the place.

We always conduct a walkthrough before we investigate a place. Here at the Spalding Inn, the bar area—which is under construction—seems free of ghostly activity.

After our walkthrough, it's a whole different story—at first. See all the orbs? They're actually just dust kicked up by our walking through the room.

We stand ready to go wherever our investigations take us—from private homes to public places.

George called T.A.P.S. in January 2001. Intrigued, Grant and I drove down and investigated the Clendennon residence a few days later. It was a two-level Cape Cod, the kind of house you see a lot in New England.

The Clendennons were nice people. But they weren't happy about what was going on in their home. You could tell that right off the bat. They looked as if they had been under a lot of stress.

We sat down and talked with both of them, though George was the one who answered most of our questions. After all, he was the one who had seen the female figure. His wife hadn't had any experiences at all. In fact, she didn't see the point of our conducting an investigation in her house, though she was willing to go along with it strictly for her husband's sake.

Eventually, George went to a friend's house for the night, to keep from—as he put it—"complicating the situation." Mostly, he wanted to see if the entity he had encountered would appear to us in his absence. If it did, he would know he wasn't seeing things, and hearing them as well.

I continued to talk with Deborah down in the kitchen while Grant began to set up a video camera in the upstairs bedroom. He was almost finished when he saw Deborah enter the room. She asked him a couple of questions and expressed a couple of concerns, and then—apparently satisfied—left him to his work. When Grant was finished, he rejoined me in the kitchen to apprise me of his conversation with Deborah.

As he spoke, I felt a chill climb my spine. It must have showed in my expression, because Grant asked me what was wrong. I told him I had been speaking with Deborah the whole time he was upstairs, and that she had left the kitchen just a few seconds before he joined me.

We looked at each other. "I was speaking to a doppelganger," Grant concluded. I nodded. It was the only explanation.

Those figures George had glimpsed from time to time? They were supernatural manifestations outwardly identical to his wife in every way. Inwardly, of course, they were completely different. They had no souls, no personalities, none of the intangibles that make us who we are.

Having never encountered a doppelganger before, Grant and I didn't know how such a thing manifested or why. However, we hoped that we would see this one again. As it turned out, we weren't disappointed. It made its presence felt on several more occasions that night, sometimes appearing to one of us while the other was talking with the real Deborah Clendennon. Naturally, the question arose as to which was which.

After a while, we picked up some clues. For instance, one of the Deborahs refused to touch anything. I asked her for a glass of water and she told me to help myself. Then I asked her to sign some paperwork and she told me she would get to it later.

Also, our encounters with the doppelganger tended to be short—thirty seconds at most. The real Deborah, on the other hand, could be engaged in conversation indefinitely. This observation gave us another tool to work with as we tried to distinguish one of them from the other.

Identifying the problem was definitely a step in the right direction. But we still didn't know how to resolve it. And

Deborah, who was convinced now of the doppelganger's existence, definitely wanted the thing out of her house. She didn't like the idea of living with a supernatural entity one bit, especially when it looked just like her.

George, for his part, was still a bit of a skeptic. He had brought us in because he understood there was more to his situation than met the eye. He had caught glimpses of a mysterious figure. But he couldn't wrap his head around the idea that it was a spitting image of his wife, or that it could actually carry on a conversation.

Back in Rhode Island, Grant and I brainstormed all week. One thing we wanted to do was prove to George that he had a doppelganger on his hands. The other was to rid the Clendennons of their houseguest.

Finally, we decided to try to bring the two Deborahs together, face to face. We didn't know for sure if that would solve the problem, but at least it would prove that something paranormal was going on. If George was there when the two Deborahs met, all the better. But it seemed like a lot to coordinate his presence at such a confrontation, so we made that part of it a low priority.

The problem was that Grant and I couldn't stay in communication, even by walkie-talkie, for fear of scaring off the doppelganger. So we set up a schedule. Every half hour, we would meet in the Clendennons' bedroom, doing our best to take a Deborah along with us. Eventually, we were bound to wind up with two Deborahs.

On our next visit to the Clendennon residence, we put our plan into action. Before long, we got the feeling that the real Deborah was downstairs and the fake one was upstairs. So Grant hung around upstairs until he ran into the fake one. Then he engaged her in conversation while gradually maneuvering himself in front of the door to the room. If she was going to leave, she would have to go through him.

Right on schedule, I brought the real Deborah up to the bedroom. But right before we could enter, the fake Deborah looked distressed and mentioned to Grant that she would be right back. Then she opened another door and left the room—just as I walked in with the real Deborah. Grant looked exasperated and said that the doppelganger had been there a couple of seconds earlier. Unfortunately, she had opened another door to the room and gone through it.

Deborah told us that the other woman couldn't have left the room that way. Then she opened it and showed us why. That door just led into a clothes closet. There was no room beyond it.

It was a frustrating night. We had come within a hair of forcing the two Deborahs to confront each other. Still, the tactic had a positive effect, because the doppelganger never showed itself in the Clendennon household again.

GHOST HUNTER'S MANUAL: WHY AT NIGHT?

We are often asked why we conduct our investigations at night. Is it just that we like to rummage around in dark places? Hardly. We would much rather rummage around under conditions in which we can see, and maybe save some of what's left of the flesh covering our shins.

So why do we spend so much time in the dark? The main reason is that our infrared cameras work best in the dark. On those rare occasions when we catch anomalies, we pick up either a shadowy figure or a faint light. To maximize our chances of detecting these phenomena, we try to operate in lightless conditions and depend on the infrared part of the spectrum as much as possible. The other issue is that paranormal activity most often manifests itself after dusk, especially between the hours of 11:00 P.M. and 4:00 A.M. But that raises another question: Why do spirits choose those hours over any others?

The explanation turns on the notion that supernatural entities need energy to make themselves visible. That's why we look for energy fluctuations when we're investigating a potential haunting. When a spirit is trying to manifest, it sucks up all the ambient energy in the area.

During the day, when there's a lot of competing light, supernatural entities require a whole lot of energy to get themselves noticed. At night, when it's dark out, they require much less energy. Think of a spirit as a flashlight. During the day, you may hardly notice it's on. But at night, it can be visible from miles around.

At any given point in time, there may be untold numbers of human spirits trying to make their presence felt by the living. But their greatest chance of success is at night, which is why they are seen and heard at that time—and why we end up looking for them in the wee hours.

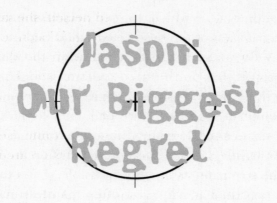

Jason: Our Biggest Regret

2001

We're not perfect here at T.A.P.S. We make mistakes, some of them the kind that keep us up long into the night, thinking coulda-woulda-shoulda. In the end, all we can do is our best, and when we make a mistake, do our damnedest to correct it.

On Monday, July 16, at about three in the afternoon, we got a call from a woman in St. Charles, a town of about a thousand people in Ontario, Canada. The woman, April Singer, was reporting threatening activity in her home. In a voice that reeked of nervousness, she said she had been attacked on numerous occasions by an unseen force. Usually, these attacks took place in the bathroom while she was either bathing or sitting on the toilet.

April, who described herself as being in her midthirties, said that she had been grabbed in what she called "sexual ways." Afterward, when she examined herself, she saw burn marks in the places where she felt she had been touched. What's more, handprints would turn up on the bathroom mirror—but not on the outside, where they could be wiped off. They would show up *inside* the mirror.

Her dog, a bull terrier, wouldn't enter the bathroom for anything. No matter how much she coaxed him, he would just sit and whine at the bathroom door. That scared her as much as anything else.

It was clear to us that April was upset. Unfortunately, in those days we didn't have the financial wherewithal to pick up and fly to Canada on short notice. We promised her that we would get her some help with her problem, and got on the phone looking for a paranormal group in her area.

We found a couple, too. However, none of them would return our calls, even though I let them know we might be dealing with something serious. We sent emails, but those weren't returned either.

And even if they had been, we couldn't say how professionally these groups would have handled April's case. Would they know what to do to help her? Or would they just scare her even more than she was already?

We called April back and told her that we'd had no luck, but that we would keep trying. We also asked her to remain in contact with us and let us know if the activity in her home was getting worse. She agreed that she would do that.

Unfortunately, we still couldn't obtain any local help for her. We spoke to her a couple more times over a two-week span. Then she stopped calling, and we figured she had finally received some assistance.

The next we heard of her was about a month later, at the end of August. Just after dinner, I received a phone call from a woman named Jessie Singer, who said she was April's sister. In a flat, emotionless voice, she demanded to know why her sister had called me.

Now, we don't give out information on our clients. We consider what we say to them and do for them a private matter, strictly between us and them. But I made an exception when Jessie Singer told me she was trying to retrace her sister's last steps, and had noticed a number of calls to my number made from her sister's phone.

"Last steps?" I said, feeling a pit open in my stomach.

Jessie Singer informed me that her sister April had been found dead in her bathtub on Tuesday, August 14. Apparently, April had hit her forehead on the porcelain sink, fallen into the tub a full eight feet away, and drowned.

Now I understood why Jessie Singer had been so terse with me. I told her what her sister had been calling us about, and that I had been working for a while on getting her some help. I asked if there had been any marks on her sister's body, burn marks, for example. She said that there was a mark over April's left breast that looked like a cigar burn. However, she added, April had been a smoker and could have caused the damage herself.

However April had died, I felt bad about it. And I felt worse when Jessie said, "It would have been nice if you had actually helped her." Then I heard her hang up the phone on me.

But the April Singer case wasn't over—at least, not for me. It continued to eat at me over the years, long after I heard the grim details of her death. I couldn't help thinking that what happened to her could have been avoided. If there had been a reliable paranormal group up in Ontario, they might have done something. She might still have been alive today.

In fact, this client's sad end was one of the reasons I created the T.A.P.S. family of paranormal investigators—a network of groups across the world that observes the same professional standards as T.A.P.S. itself, and can get timely assistance to people almost anywhere. Unfortunately for April Singer, that network didn't exist back in 2001.

It does now.

Grant: A Little Help from My Friends

2001

Vickie Schizzano, a single, middle-aged woman who lived in an upscale townhouse in eastern Connecticut, had a small group of close friends who would take turns inviting everyone over to their homes. When Vickie visited her friends' places, she would share a peaceful, diverting evening with them. But when it was Vickie's turn to entertain, the evening was anything but peaceful.

She and her friends would be interrupted by one bizarre sound after another—a soft moaning, a thin, distant screaming, and a steady series of thumps that could be heard throughout the house. At first, she just found the sounds inconvenient. But as time went on and Vickie couldn't come up with an explanation for them, she became more than inconvenienced.

She became downright frightened.

After all, Vickie's friends had convinced her that the sounds were of paranormal origin. They unanimously insisted that she have her house scoured for evidence of ghostly activity. And because one of them had heard of T.A.P.S., they asked Jay and me to conduct the investigation.

When we arrived at Vickie's townhouse, we found not only her but also a half dozen of her friends on hand. Normally we keep our investigations as private as possible, so we asked Vickie if she was comfortable speaking in her friends' presence.

"Very comfortable," she told us emphatically. "In fact, I insist on it."

If it was okay with her, it was okay with us. She went on to describe what she had experienced. Whenever she mentioned one of the sounds, her friends would take the opportunity to elaborate on it.

"It's not just a moaning," said one of them, making a face.

"More like a groaning," said another one.

"Like someone's in pain," said a third friend.

"*Terrible* pain," said a fourth.

Their comments grew even more histrionic when we got to the screaming they'd heard. It went from occasional to continuous, from distant to painfully close, and from faint to blood-curdling. The thumping was likened to someone knocking on a door, beating a drum, and hammering a nail—and Vickie, who was obviously a bit too influenced by her friends, agreed with each and every description.

Fortunately, they all told the same basic story. As far as

we could tell, it all sounded potentially debunkable. The sounds could have been the products of grouchy heating pipes, unfastened shutters, or a loose joist.

Still, we wouldn't know for certain until we investigated, so that's what we did. The first night, we failed to collect any evidence whatsoever, either documentation or personal experiences. It wasn't until the second night, around one-thirty in the morning, that we got some results.

As Vickie and her friends had claimed, there was a steady knocking sound that came and went. It was joined after a while by a faint moaning and eventually a couple of screams as well. Fortunately, we managed to get them all on audiotape.

Vickie was happy to hear that we were able to confirm her experiences. No doubt, her friends would be happy too. However, we still couldn't say where the sounds had come from. We hoped we would know more after we reviewed our data.

Back in Warwick, Jay and I listened to the sounds on our audiotapes over and over again, all through the afternoon. It wasn't until dinnertime that we finally developed a theory about what was going on. Sitting back in our chairs, we looked at each other.

"You think that's what it is?" I asked.

Jay shrugged. "Only one way to find out."

Contacting Vickie, we asked for permission to come over one more time. Of course, she agreed. When we got there, around ten o'clock on a Friday night, all her friends were present as well. Everyone wanted to hear what we had discovered.

We didn't tell them anything right away. We just led the

entourage into Vickie's bedroom, turned on our tape recorder, and waited. Vickie and her friends speculated like crazy, but none of them guessed what we were doing.

As it got later, we began to give them more information. We pointed out that our previous visit to Vickie's townhouse had been on a Friday night as well. Clearly, we were trying to duplicate as closely as possible the circumstances under which we recorded the ghostly sounds.

This time, we didn't have to wait as long to hear them. At about a quarter to one, the thumping started. It seemed to be coming from Vickie's bedroom wall—or more accurately, what was on the other side of it—because we could feel the vibration under our fingertips. After a while, we heard moaning as well. And then the screams, which—as we listened this time—sounded more like screams of pleasure than screams of pain.

"Oh, my God," said Vickie, as understanding dawned.

As it turned out, her neighbor was a young man with an active sex life. On Friday nights, he would go to a club, bring home a woman, and have sex with her. The thumping was the sound of his headboard hitting the wall.

In another townhouse community, it might have been easier for us to identify the source of the sounds. However, in Vickie's development, the walls were pretty thick. It was harder to tell where the sounds were coming from.

The next day, we knocked on the door of Vickie's neighbor, told him who we were, and asked him if he wouldn't mind tightening up his headboard and moving his bed to another wall. He was a good sport about it and did as we asked. After that, the thumping in Vickie's place stopped.

Though, as she informed us when we checked back

with her a few weeks later, the moans and the screaming continued—much to the amusement of her friends, who knew now they weren't listening to ghosts.

GHOST HUNTER'S MANUAL: MATRIXING

Ever sit back in the grass on a summer night and consider the face of the man in the moon? As you know, there's no face up there. What you're seeing is the configuration of craters and ravines that marks the moon's surface. It's only your mind's natural tendency to find something familiar in complex sets of shapes or colors that makes you think you're looking at a face.

The same thing happens when you're looking a photograph—maybe one you took in the course of a paranormal investigation. You're looking at some tree branches, and you see a child among them. Or you're looking into a cluttered closet and you see a leering skull. Or you're looking into a mirror and you see a face looking back at you from over your shoulder.

More than likely, there's neither a child, a skull, nor a face in these photographs. Your mind is constructing them out of the information available to it. We at T.A.P.S. have a name for this phenomenon. We call it "matrixing."

If it weren't for matrixing, we wouldn't be able to function in the world. We wouldn't be able to recognize our friends and families, our houses, or our cars. In fact, it is due to the effects of matrixing that we are able to identify letters in varying type fonts. If our minds weren't able to take the subtle nuances of each letter and make something familiar out of them, we would only be able to read one font.

Matrixing applies to our sense of hearing as well. You can hear a random noise and mistake it for something familiar. That's because your mind is working hard to turn it into something recognizable.

Unfortunately, matrixing can be a hindrance to us in our work as ghost hunters. In analyzing the evidence that is presented to us, we need to be objective. Otherwise, we're not doing anybody a favor—not our client, not ourselves, and not the field of paranormal investigation. We need to look at what appears to be a demonic face or a full-body apparition in a photograph, and ask ourselves if it's really there, or if it's just our minds playing tricks on us.

There are a few ways to identify matrixing and eliminate it—before someone else does, and ruins your credibility in the process. First, take a look at the type of photograph you're analyzing. Pictures of trees, fields, cluttered closets, mirrors, and glass surfaces are prime candidates for matrixing issues. They include very complex shapes and patterns, and therefore spur the mind to construct a face or body out of something that isn't there.

Second, examine the potential face or figure. If it is truly something paranormal it will be made up of its own material, not the material around it. For example, let's say you've got a picture of a forest, and you think you see a face in it. Check to see if the face is made up of the branches and leaves in the picture, or if it's independent of the branches and leaves.

Third, consider the face or figure you've captured in terms of its proportions. If it's a face, are the features "cartoony" and out of proportion to each other, or are they realistic? Does it look like something you would see in life or something someone drew in an animation studio?

You don't need art training to figure this out (although it doesn't hurt). Just go to any art supply store and pick up a book that explains proportions. Then examine the face in your photograph to see if it looks realistic or not.

There's an increasing tendency, it seems, for ghost hunters to fall prey to matrixing in their eagerness to come up with evidence of the supernatural. Don't succumb to it. Consider the possibility that your discovery is the result of matrixing before you present it to the world, and help us all gain more respect for the field of paranormal investigation.

Jason: The Child

2001

Lots of children have invisible friends, so five-year-old Justin Wilenski wasn't unusual in that regard. He had been talking with his unseen pal for the last year or so, ever since he and his parents, Peter and Rachel, had moved into their two-bedroom apartment on the second floor of a building in Hartford, Connecticut.

At first, the Wilenskis didn't mind Justin's imaginary companion. In fact, they hardly gave the matter a second thought. Then things around their apartment began disappearing—packs of cigarettes, a hand cloth, and after a while even some of the family's good silverware.

When they asked Justin about the disappearances, he said at first that he didn't know anything about them. Then he began wondering out loud whether his friend had anything to do with it. That's when his parents started realizing there might be more to the situation than met the eye.

The Wilenskis' suspicions grew stronger one day when they heard the noise of running feet in the apartment, the kind a child might make. But they couldn't find anyone responsible for the sound—not even Justin, who was away on a play date. That night, they saw a strange light appear in Justin's darkened bedroom. Naturally, they checked it out as quickly as they could. But, though they gave the room a thorough going-over, they failed to find the source of the illumination.

The same things happened again later in the week. And then again, until they gradually became regular occurrences. On top of that, Justin's toys began turning themselves on at night, until the Wilenskis were forced to remove their batteries.

Most bizarre of all was the handprint Rachel found one morning on the bathroom mirror, after she had steamed the room up with her shower. It was the size of a child's hand, but it wasn't Justin's—she was sure of that. And to her dismay, it was inside the surface of the mirror rather than on the outside.

Justin's relationship with his imaginary friend didn't seem to change through all this, but his parents began looking at it differently. Somehow, they felt, it was the key to the tide of bizarre incidents that had swept over them.

By the time they contacted us at T.A.P.S., they were in a panic, afraid their home was haunted and that Justin was at risk. Both Grant and I are fathers, so we absolutely hate the idea of a child being in danger. We put together an investigative team as quickly as we could, packed up our van, and made our way down to Hartford.

Peter and Rachel couldn't have been happier to see us. Justin was just shy, clinging to his mom's leg. As Grant and Ed set up our equipment around the apartment, keying in on all the trouble spots the Wilenskis had mentioned over the phone, Brittney and I sat down to talk with the family.

We told them what we planned to do and how we planned to do it. We said that we would try to be as unobtrusive as possible when it came to Justin. However, a lot of the activity the family had reported had taken place in his room, so we would have to apply a large portion of our efforts there.

Once we were set up, we waited for results. To our surprise, because these things often take a long time, we didn't have to wait long. In the bathroom, where we had turned on the shower, a small handprint appeared.

It was pretty distinct, and its size suggested that it had been made by a child, as Rachel had said. Also, it was very definitely located on the inside of the mirror. We took pictures of it, recorded our observations, and continued with our investigation.

For a while, nothing else happened. Then, as Brittney and I sat talking with the Wilenskis in their living room, we heard what sounded like footsteps. They seemed to be coming from the kitchen. But when we got there, there was no one in evidence and the sound had stopped.

Later on, maybe an hour later, we heard the footsteps again—quick and light, the kind a child would make. As before, the sounds seemed to be coming from the kitchen.

But our luck was no better the second time than the first. By the time we traced the footsteps to their source, whoever—or whatever—had made them was gone.

We had several cameras going, trying to pick up the light the Wilenskis had noticed in Justin's room. Unfortunately, the light never made an appearance. We speculated that what Rachel and Peter had noticed was the glint of reflected light coming from somewhere else in the house.

One of Justin's toys—with its batteries back in for the sake of our investigation—did make noise briefly. However, it was designed with a visual sensor to respond to the approach of certain objects, so it might simply have had a wire crossed. We didn't see it as evidence of paranormal activity.

But when we considered the whole situation, we had to admit the possibility that there was something supernatural going on. We shared our thinking with the Wilenskis. They seemed to take it in stride, though it must have been a bit of a shock to them.

The next morning, Ed and Brittney visited Town Hall and the local library to see if they could shed any light on what we had seen and heard. Nothing turned up. But Grant and I, who went knocking on doors elsewhere in the building, had some luck.

One of the older residents, who had been there a long time, spoke of a fire that had burned down part of the building many years earlier. There had been three fatalities—two adults and a child. Grant and I thanked the old fellow for his time and shared the information with the Wilenskis later that evening.

They were saddened by what they heard, so much so that Rachel started to cry. Grant and I understood. No one likes to hear about a young life cut short by tragedy, least of all people who have kids themselves.

"Under the circumstances," Grant said in his usual gentle manner, "we believe the little boy's spirit is present in this apartment. Most likely, he's the one responsible for everything that's been going on. If you want, we can talk about strategies for getting rid of him. If he left, it would put a stop to all the activity."

But, as I had suspected, the Wilenskis didn't want to push out the young spirit. They said they would be happy to let him stay, and that they would contact us again if the activity seemed to become a problem.

Obviously it didn't, because we haven't heard from them since.

GHOST HUNTER'S MANUAL: ORBS

As paranormal investigators, we may be a little too eager sometimes to capture evidence on film. In our drive to provide documentation, we will embrace a supernatural explanation when there's a perfectly good natural one available. Nowhere is this truer than in the area of orbs, which have been a lightning rod for controversy in the world of ghost hunters over the years.

There are four possible reasons for an orb to appear in a video or photographic image. One is that the orb is simply light reflecting off a dust particle. In fact, the tiniest particle of dust may reflect the flash of a still camera or the infrared light of a digital camera, producing a round ball of light stunning enough for most investigators to drool over. Your job is to keep from drooling, to remain utterly objective, and to seek out a more mundane explanation.

No doubt, you'll hear some investigators say, "But none of the other images had orbs in them. Only this one." That's because this was the only one in which a particle of dust caught the light of the camera flash at just the right angle. The dust is almost certainly present in the other photos, but it's not in a position to reflect light.

So how do we know when it is dust and when it is a true paranormal phenomenon? Dust tends to refract in a perfect circle, with little "noise" in it, and no border. It looks like a cell inspected under a microscope.

Moisture is another condition that can make orbs appear in a recorded image. Fortunately, orbs caused by moisture are easier to spot. They tend to have angular sides, and they fade from solid to transparent. As with orbs caused by dust, they have no border. And like the dust particle, moisture can appear in one photo and not in another, even if the second one was taken immediately afterward.

The larger the particle of moisture, the less angular it will look in a photo. A picture of raindrops will yield very little angularity at all. In fact it will show you small, solid-looking objects that can easily be mistaken for supernaturally created orbs. A fine mist, by contrast, will produce orbs with very angular sides.

A third cause of orb-type images is light reflecting off an object in the picture. This is undoubtedly the most common source of mistaken photo analyses. It's also the easiest one to spot. If you have an image with multiple orbs in it, and one is more intense than the others, chances are good that you have a reflection.

Here's why. When light reflects off an object, it produces a number of circular "flares" in a photographic image. These vary in intensity, and are usually located along a straight line emanating from the source, which is usually some small object in the background that is overlooked by the investigator reviewing the photo. This object can range from a small ring on a nightstand to the varnish on a table or door.

If you have Adobe Photoshop, there's a way to see if this is the cause of your orb. Just take your image, run its gamma to near max, and check out the orb's gamma signature. If it's just a reflection from an object somewhere in the picture, that object will have the same gamma signature as the orb.

The last possible cause of an orb is true paranormal energy. If you've captured an orb in your image and ruled out all the other ways it could have appeared, you may have yourself a real prize. Now it's time to take a closer look at it, to confirm that it's what you think it is.

What you're looking for is a solid object that emits its own light, rather than reflecting light from something else. On film, it looks like a Ping-Pong ball that's been thrown across the screen. If it has a sign of movement, such as a blurred trail behind it, congratulations are in order: You've got what we at T.A.P.S. would call viable evidence of paranormal activity.

Grant:
A Sister's Feelings

2002

We've all heard the expression "my brother's keeper." It dates back to the Old Testament and the story of Jacob and Esau. When it comes to the paranormal, it has an even deeper meaning. And it doesn't have to be brothers we're talking about. More often than not, it's about sisters.

The case I'm thinking of came to us early in the year. I was contacted by a friend, Dana Marino, who lived in eastern Massachusetts, not far from the Rhode Island border. Dana and her husband, Jerry, were scared for their two daughters, sixteen-year-old Mara and nine-year-old Suzanne. Their daughter Mara had become a different person over the previous few months. At times, she just seemed a little out of touch with reality. At other times, she became mean, and at still others she was depressed.

But it was little Suzanne whom the Marinos were really worried about. Dana said that Suzanne was plagued by demons—fierce ones that would laugh at her and scratch her body. Jay and I spoke with Suzanne and she admitted it was true. She told us that she often heard voices in her head, and when that happened she couldn't even find her way out of her own bedroom. The voices would make fun of her, and after they were gone she would always find scratch marks in her skin.

We worked with the family for some time, conducting investigations weekend after weekend, trying to determine what was going on. After a while, we started to develop a theory. We were still puzzling it out when we got a desperate phone call from the Marino family.

Fortunately, we were only half an hour away. We arrived to find little Suzanne in a fit of rage. She was tossing chairs and even tables around the house, the kind a grown man might not have been able to throw. At one point she even began pushing a heavy piano toward her father.

The girl couldn't have weighed more than sixty pounds. Her arms were like pipe cleaners. And yet she was immensely strong. Her voice was deeper than it had a right to be and her speech was strewn with obscenities. She spoke of her "master" and babbled on about matters that made no sense to us. There was a horrid stench in the room, a smell like a very bad dirty diaper, and every so often Suzanne's body would spasm as if it were caught in the grip of unseen forces.

Which, apparently, it was.

It wasn't the first time we had encountered a case of possession, and unfortunately it wouldn't be the last.

Suzanne's fit had all the earmarks—the smell, the uncontrollable fury, the cursing, the unbelievable strength. Luckily, the Marinos had also called for help from some neighbors, two members of their church. With their assistance, Jay and I were able to restrain the little girl—if only barely. She tried to escape with every tool she had at her disposal, kicking and biting and screaming until her throat was raw, but we held on.

The two neighbors had apparently had experience with cases of possession. They knew what kind of prayers to say and what ceremonies to conduct, quoting from the New Testament and calling on God, Jesus, his angels, the Virgin Mary, and the apostles to drive evil from their midst. After what seemed like forever, Suzanne shivered and fell into a deep, peaceful sleep.

But she wouldn't remain in a tranquil state for long. Not unless we got to the bottom of what was happening at the Marino house. Dana and Jerry had seen Suzanne seized by fits of anger before, but those prior episodes had never been anywhere near as severe as this one. They were in tears over their daughter's plight, feeling helpless against it.

Jay and I were exhausted from wrestling with Suzanne, our shirts soaked through with perspiration. Sitting down with the Marinos, we told them about our suspicions. They didn't want to believe us at first, but eventually came to see the evidence the way we did.

Some time later, Mara came home from her friend's house, where she had spent the day. She turned ashen when she learned of what had happened. However, she didn't comment on it, and looked as if she were hiding something.

She finally confessed after Jay and I told her about our theory. After all, demonic entities don't simply enter a home on their own. They have to be invited to do so, either purposely or by accident.

In a quiet voice, Mara confessed that she didn't like her little sister. She said she had taken part in dark rituals in which she would use her sister as an offering to gain certain things, both material and intangible. By the dark entities' standards Mara had "ownership" over her younger sister because Mara was older, and the older or more powerful member of a household is responsible for all the younger or less powerful members.

Dana and Jerry were aghast. However, it was clear to them now what had happened. They accepted it, but they still didn't know what to do about it.

An exorcism could free Suzanne from the supernatural entities who had taken hold of her. However, her possession was the result of some deep rifts between the sisters, which had been made worse by Mara's choice of friends. Jay and I suggested that the family move to another town to get a fresh start for their daughters. Fortunately, Jerry had a job that allowed for that. In time, Mara benefited from the change of scenery and was able to turn her life around.

Suzanne, meanwhile, was subjected to a rite of exorcism by a Catholic priest, who succeeded in freeing her from the entity possessing her. She hasn't had any problems of that nature since. And just as important, she found it in her heart to forgive Mara for what she had done to her.

Why do possessions occur? That's not an easy question to answer, although lots of paranormal investigators have tried to do so. However, one explanation seems to make sense to us.

For reasons beyond our understanding, demons—that is, supernatural entities intent on doing harm in the world—don't have the ability to take a human life on their own. So what they do instead is attempt to possess a person, whether man or woman, child or adult, and use that person as a tool to achieve their objective. They stir up fear, misery, and chaos, do damage and cause injury, and even commit acts of murder—all without breaking the cosmic law that keeps them in their place.

It's a loophole in the contract made millennia ago by God and the Devil. At least, that's how we look at it. Your mileage may vary.

How do these entities obtain control of their hosts? In every case we have ever investigated, they obtain the cooperation of a human being—either the victim or someone close to the victim. And if that's so, it's our fault that possessions take place.

After all, we have free will. We can give supernatural beings access to us or we can shut them out. The choice is ours.

Often, people are possessed when they're at their weakest. Maybe their will power has been compromised by addiction to drugs or alcohol. Maybe they've had a traumatic experience, such as an incident of sexual or physical abuse. Maybe they just suffer from low self-esteem.

Any one of these possibilities gives the inhuman entity the opening it needs. But possession doesn't happen overnight. It's usually a series of attacks by the entity that ultimately breaks down its host and gives it entry.

Children are an exception to the rule that people are to blame for possessions. If they're targeted by a demonic entity and tricked into doing something they shouldn't, it's clearly not their fault. They're too innocent to know what they're doing, too naïve in the ways of good and evil.

A child will play with an invisible friend and not feel the least bit threatened. But that invisible friend could be an inhuman spirit, slowly but surely taking advantage of the situation. Before anyone knows what's going on, the child is possessed.

Probably the best-known case of possession is the one dramatized in the movie *The Exorcist,* based on the book by William Peter Blatty, which packed theaters across the country back in 1973. In the movie, it was a twelve-year-old girl named Regan who was possessed by a demonic entity. But in real life, it was a fourteen-year-old boy from Mount Rainier, Maryland, a small town not far from Washington, D.C. Back in 1949, the boy was freed from his possession by a Catholic priest, who used an ancient practice described by several religions as "an exorcism."

Naturally, the movie producers had to exaggerate the

details of the story for the sake of ticket sales, so they had Regan do a few things no human being has ever done—not even in the deepest throes of a demonic possession. It's a scary thing to see someone under the control of a supernatural entity, no question about it, but even we have never heard of a victim's head spinning around on her shoulders.

Under the right circumstances, anyone can be possessed by a demon. It doesn't have to be a Catholic—although, thanks to *The Exorcist,* it's the Catholic Church that's most closely identified with the concept of demonic possession. In fact, the victim can be someone who doesn't believe in God or the Devil at all. A refusal to believe is no defense when it comes to the supernatural.

However, it is a liability in terms of exorcising the demon, because the one thing you need if you're going to benefit from an exorcism is faith. It doesn't even seem to matter *which* faith. You can be a Catholic, a Protestant, a Jew, a Muslim, even a pagan—you just have to believe in *something.*

Let's get something straight—there is no way for a human being to destroy a demonic entity. They have been around for millennia and we would be naïve to think we have the power to put an end to any of them. Of course, with the help of clergy, we can successfully expel them from their human playgrounds, driving them out of the bodies they have come to possess.

But even then, there's a price to pay, and not an insignificant one. You see, when you work on a possession case, the demon you're working against knows who you are. If you encounter him a second time, he will recognize you. And if one demon knows you, they *all* know you.

On the other hand, we can't just let them have their way with their human hosts. That's something neither of us would ever consider. Okay, so we're bulletin-board fodder in some demon locker room; it's not a comforting thought, but we live with it. You might say it comes with the territory.

Jason: Piece by Piece

2002

Ben Forth was a contractor in central Connecticut who bought an old farmhouse as a fixer-upper. He figured that with his expertise in carpentry and other trades, he could turn the house, which was built in the 1800s next to an apple orchard, into something he could never have afforded otherwise.

It seemed like a good strategy. Unfortunately, like a lot of good strategies, it ran into some complications.

By the time Ben contacted T.A.P.S., he was a severely frustrated man. Apparently, he had been seeing apparitions almost since the day he moved in. And always the same apparitions, over and over again.

Sometimes he would be standing near the staircase that led from the main foyer to the second floor, his mind on something else, and he would hear a noise. Turning without thinking, just as a reflex, he would see the figure of a woman tripping and falling down the stairs. It happened every day, sometimes several times.

On other occasions, Ben would hear the thumping sound of someone running around on his porch. Then there would be a banging on the front door, and—as he went to open it—a boy's voice demanding to come inside because he was freezing. What's more, Ben couldn't just stand there and let it happen. He had to go to the door in case there was someone flesh and blood out there.

Ben had never been the timid sort. He was a big, strapping guy with powerful hands who didn't back away from confrontations. But he couldn't stand the thought of living with the apparitions any longer.

At his request, Grant and I took a team to the farmhouse and conducted an investigation. We set up cameras at the foot of the stairs and on the porch, as well as elsewhere in the house. As it turned out, we didn't have any personal experiences, which was a source of great annoyance to Ben. After all, he had them all the time.

However, when we returned to Rhode Island and went over our data, we caught a very distinct EVP. It was a woman's scream, thin and high-pitched and laced with fright, followed by what sounded like someone falling down a set of stairs. When we told Ben what we had captured, he breathed a sigh of relief.

"That's exactly what I've been hearing," he told us.

We went back to the farmhouse on several other occasions. Besides the EVP of the woman falling down the stairs, we caught another one of a boyish voice saying, "Please, please, I will die from the cold." Both of them came up on our audiotapes during more than one investigation.

Finally, we saw that we were collecting the same EVPs but nothing else, so we stopped visiting Ben's farmhouse. At that point, we began the research phase of our investigation. Our goal was to identify the woman on the stairs and the boy out on the porch.

Despite our best efforts, we couldn't make any headway. Still, it was clear that the people represented in the apparitions had experienced some kind of trauma—maybe even death. Based on the evidence we had collected, which indicated that the paranormal activity was of a repetitive nature, we had to say the farmhouse was the site of a residual haunting.

That meant there was no easy way to get rid of it. It was tied to the house, or some aspect of the house, and always would be. We advised Ben to learn to live with the sounds, or else abandon his fixer-upper project and move elsewhere.

The only other course of action was a really tricky one—to find the material the residual energy was trapped in and remove it from the premises. Ben said there was no way he was going to move away, but he had no idea which pieces of the house contained the energy. So he began removing them one by one.

He started with the bric-a-brac, but the apparitions kept coming. Next he replaced the rugs left on the floors. Still no change. Taking out the tables and chairs didn't seem to solve the problem either.

Ben didn't stop. He threw out the interior doors. Then he got rid of the cupboards and stripped away the wallpaper. He tore away the moldings, pulled out the sink, and trashed the fireplace. He even replaced the light fixtures with new ones.

But nothing worked. Eventually, Ben started ripping out the structural elements of the house. The stairs down which the woman seemed to be falling? Gone. The porch on which the boy could be heard running? Gone as well.

And still he kept hearing the same ghostly sounds, until he thought he would go out of his mind. So he kept tearing up the farmhouse, hoping he would finally eliminate whatever held the residual energy.

The roof came off, section by section. The windows were smashed and thrown away. Rooms were gutted. Floors were pried loose, board by board.

When we saw how far Ben had gone in his quest, we urged him to get a grip on himself. But he couldn't stop. Eventually he ended up knocking down the whole house and building an entirely new one in its place.

At long last, the activity stopped. Ben's farmhouse was gone as if it had never been there in the first place, but he had won his battle with the residual haunting.

GHOST HUNTER'S MANUAL: RESIDUAL HAUNTINGS

The most common variety of haunting is what we call "residual." A residual haunting is like a loop in a video recording. An event that originally had some significance to someone is played over and over again ad infinitum, giving an observer the impression that the figures involved are lost in a time warp.

However, the people we see or hear in a residual haunting aren't supernatural spirits. They have no awareness of themselves, their surroundings, or those who might be observing them. They can't communicate with each other or anyone else. In a way, they are like the characters in a movie. They can't step outside their roles to interact with the audience.

Residual hauntings typically originate with a violent or traumatic event. This is why they so often involve screaming or crying. Observers may also hear the sounds of footsteps on stairs or in hallways, as such sounds often preceded or resulted from the event in question.

A residual haunting may also be set in motion by a series of events, as long as they were regularly repeated and had an emotional impact on someone. It is this impact that creates a field of paranormal energy, which we perceive in the form of sounds, sights, and sometimes even smells. The energy always appears to attach itself to a particular building or location, which is why a residual haunting seems to manifest itself over and over again in the same place, if not always at the same time. What's more, its frequency can vary wildly. It can occur every night, every week, or just once a year.

There is very little a paranormal investigator can do about this style of haunting except help his clients understand what is going on in their home and explain that the phenomenon poses no danger to them. After all, the energy that gives rise to it is not controlled by the person who left it behind. There is no intent behind the event, malevolent or otherwise.

Of course, a family coping with a residual haunting may not be comforted by this information. Despite the impersonal nature of the phenomenon, it can still be a frightening and emotionally draining experience for people exposed to it night in and night out. Sometimes the knowledge that it is coming is worse than the event itself. In the end, those affected by a residual haunting need to accept what is happening and learn to deal with it, or move on.

Grant:
All Too Familiar

2002

Usually the contacts we receive on our website are from individuals who believe they are experiencing the paranormal. However, we are sometimes called in by people whose friends or relatives are the ones having the experiences. In this case, it was a woman asking for help on an old friend's behalf.

Her friend, Anita Ormont, was a single, middle-aged woman who lived in a house in northern Massachusetts. Anita was slender and petite, and had probably been attractive at one time, but when we met her she looked haggard, as if she hadn't slept in a while. In fact, she hadn't. In recent weeks, she said, she had been awakened repeatedly by loud, high-pitched screams. And as she lay there in bed, too frightened to get up and figure out where the screams had come from, she heard voices. Her impression was that the voices weren't happy.

Anita had also seen the apparition of a young girl, around thirteen years old, in the house. The girl always appeared in the same situations. She was either running down the stairs, clawing at the inside of the front door, or sitting on the floor in the corner of one of the bedrooms. Anita told us that she had witnessed the activity in each location many times, but would always turn away or cover her eyes in terror. By the time she dared to look again, the girl was always gone.

She was glad that her friend had asked us for assistance. "I would have contacted you myself," she said, "but I didn't want to be labeled a crazy person." It was the sort of comment we heard often.

Because of the frequency of the activity in Anita's house, we knew we had a good chance of seeing it ourselves. We set up cameras near the stairs, by the front door, and in the bedroom in question, and began our investigation. Unfortunately, though we were in the house all night, we didn't catch anything.

Back the next weekend, we gave it another shot. Still nothing. The entire night went by without a hint of an occurrence. But we weren't about to give up—not as long as Anita had that sleepless, hollowed-out look in her eyes. Sometimes we get the feeling that a client is exaggerating his or her experiences, or even making them up altogether. That wasn't the case with Anita. We were convinced that she was telling us the truth about what she had seen.

It took several trips back and forth to Massachusetts,

but our patience was finally rewarded. We were sitting in Anita's living room, asking her how she had been since our last visit, when we heard a series of desperate screams from upstairs and then heard someone running down the staircase. By the time we got there the screaming had stopped, giving way to a different kind of sound—a distinct banging in the vicinity of the front door.

As we turned in that direction, we saw what Anita had seen—a girl about thirteen years old, with long blonde hair. But she was more like a mist than a flesh-and-blood person, fading in and out. We approached her and tried to make contact with her, but she ignored us. Then, finally, she dissipated altogether.

Obviously, the entity was incapable of perceiving us, much less responding to our attempts to communicate with it. It was simply a recurring phenomenon, devoid of awareness or intent. It was clear to us, at that point, that we were dealing with a residual haunting.

From our point of view, that was good news. Residual hauntings don't directly harm the human beings with whom they share a residence. They can be unnerving, of course, but they're not destructive.

Anita wasn't cheered in the least. She still dreaded seeing the apparition of the young girl. Sometimes our clients are relieved when we find tangible evidence of the paranormal because it validates their experiences. In Anita's case, our encounter with the entity seemed to have the opposite effect. She was more terrified than ever.

And we were even more determined to understand the origins of the haunting. The problem was that our research hadn't turned up anything useful in that regard. We hadn't read anything about a young girl being killed or dying in Anita's house. We hadn't come across anything at all that shed light on the haunting.

It was a frustrating situation. We continued to speak with Anita regularly, looking for answers. We learned that she had intensely disliked her parents. However, when they passed away, they had left her the small home she grew up in. She moved in shortly after their deaths and had lived there ever since, without incident—until now.

Soon, we had our second encounter with the entity. We were walking upstairs with Anita when we saw the thirteen-year-old girl coming down the stairs. Anita, who was a step ahead of Jason and me, froze on the spot—for once, too shocked to turn away. The girl seemed to run right through her, and then through Jason as well. But before she went all the way through Jason, she started fading away.

We continued to hear her footsteps heading for the front door. However, the girl herself was nowhere to be seen. She had vanished.

It took a while to calm Anita down after that. She was trembling, having come in contact with the entity for the first time. It had to have been a weird experience, for her even more than for Jason.

We wanted very much to comfort her, but we were running out of options. We had no record of a traumatic death in the house, and therefore no insight into the conditions that had given rise to the haunting. And we were dealing with a residual situation, which would make the entity nearly impossible to remove.

Finally, we turned to Anita's friend for hints on the best way to ease Anita's mind. After all, she had known Anita for a long time. She showed us a picture of them together when they first met, at the age of fifteen.

We looked at the picture in awe. Standing alongside Anita's friend was the spitting image of the young girl we had seen first near the front door and more recently on the stairs. Even her hair was like the entity's, long and blonde.

"That's Anita?" I asked, to make absolutely certain.

"That's Anita," she assured us.

I looked at Jason. He had come to the same conclusion I had. Given the evidence, it was the only conclusion possible: *The entity was Anita!* Not as she was now, a woman in her midforties, but as she had been when she was thirteen.

If we were right, we had witnessed something we had heard of in theory but never experienced firsthand—a living residual haunting. In most cases we had investigated, people and places were haunted by the dead. But in this case, Anita was receiving visits from her own teenaged self.

It was a staggering thought.

A few days later, we sat down with Anita and asked her if she had ever had any traumatic events in her life. She told us that she had not. Patiently, we asked her to describe the entity she had seen on the stairs that day. She described the girl in some detail. Then we showed her the picture of herself when she was young.

Jason and I watched as the waves of realization flooded over our client. Before long, the realization turned to panic. We told her it was all right, and that such a phenomenon does take place from time to time.

Like a dam breaking and releasing the pent-up fury of the river behind it, Anita started to spew forth the horrid story of her childhood. She told us how her father would beat her as she was growing up, and how on her thirteenth birthday he tried to rape her. She recalled in vivid detail the events of that night. How she had run down the stairs in terror, trying to get away from him, and how she couldn't unlock the door to escape. How he beat her and tried to have his way with her, and how she barely managed to fend him off. When he finally gave up, she had returned to her room and sat crying in a corner on the floor.

She had completely blocked out the memory. We felt bad making her live it all over again. However, once we had uncovered the truth we felt compelled to reveal it to her. She had the right to know.

To our relief, Anita's state of mind improved dramatically once she knew the origin of the entity in her home. However, she still felt uncomfortable watching herself repeat the horrible experience she had locked away so deep in her mind. Some weeks later, she told us that she had decided to make a new start, called a real estate broker, and put her house up for sale.

GHOST HUNTER'S MANUAL: CHILDREN AND GHOSTS

When there's a supernatural entity intruding in someone's household, why is it so often one of the children who becomes aware of it first? Usually, the child doesn't know what he is dealing with, thinking instead that the entity is an invisible playmate. But one way or the other, it's the youngest in the home who seems to sense the presence of something paranormal before anyone else.

Why are children so much more open to these phenomena? Because to a child, anything is possible. Santa still slides down the chimney at Christmastime, the Tooth Fairy still collects those teeth under the pillow, and the Easter Bunny still drops off baskets of eggs. Children haven't yet been conditioned by society to distinguish between what's real and what's not.

Over the years, they'll be told sternly to stop making up stories, or playing with their imaginary friends. They'll be encouraged to develop a "healthy" skepticism about anything other people can't see or hear. But when they're little, they're still receptive to a range of supernatural entities and events.

Of course, there are families who recognize that there are spirits and other things out there that we can't see. These families tend to be more accepting of their children's playing with imaginary friends. They don't attempt to change the children's ideas or make them feel self-conscious, so the children remain open to the realm of the supernatural.

More and more sensitives are popping up in the field of paranormal investigations. These are people who have been allowed to develop their talents without being told that what they saw as children wasn't real. As a result, they still have the ability to see those phenomena as adults.

But how many more sensitives might there be today if their families had allowed them to remain open to the supernatural? And as a result, how much more might we know about the "other side"?

Jason: "They're Talkin' To Me!"

2002

We at T.A.P.S. end up talking to a lot of people over the phone, some of them too rattled by their experiences to speak clearly. We try to get them to calm down, to tell us slowly and calmly what's happening to them. Usually that helps.

In the case of Jimmy Jaynes, it didn't help a bit. His voice was hoarse and he slurred his words, as if he were gargling with sandpaper. But we heard enough to know that his name was Jimmy, he was sixty-seven years old, and he was hearing voices around his house. What's more, he felt they were from "the other side."

"Please," he said, "can you help me?"

That was enough to get us packed up and on the highway. Jimmy's house was a tiny Cape Cod shoehorned into a crowded little development a couple of miles from Eaton, Connecticut. He was waiting for us on the porch, a tall, thin old man with a rumpled baseball hat, eager to share his experiences with a couple of guys who might actually believe him.

Jimmy's voice wasn't any clearer in person than it had been on the phone. He sounded as if he smoked two packs of cigarettes a day and washed it down with a fifth of vodka, but he swore that he never drank or smoked. In fact, he assured us, he didn't have any vices at all—especially the kind that would have him hearing voices.

"So," said Grant, "what do the voices sound like? Can you make out what they're saying?"

Jimmy could hear words, he was sure of that. He just couldn't string enough of them together to work out a sentence. We could tell how frustrating the whole thing was for him, how humiliating. But until we heard the words as he did, there wasn't much we could do.

Other ghost-hunting groups might have gone in there and pronounced the place haunted. However, that wasn't the way we operated. Before we raised the possibility of paranormal activity, we had to have proof—the kind that could be played back in video or audio form, or at least verified by witnesses.

"How long does it usually take before you hear something?" Grant asked.

Jimmy shrugged. "Could be minutes, could be hours. When it happens, it happens a lot, though. Nonstop, you might say."

He had piqued our curiosity. We decided to sit there at

the kitchen table with him and wait. If we were lucky, we wouldn't have to wait long.

To pass the time, we asked him about his life. It turned out that he had spent some time in Michigan. "You know," Jimmy said, "back there, we used to do a lot of ice fishing. Cold as hell, let me tell you. At the height of winter, we had to cut through eight inches of ice to—" Suddenly, he got this weird, scrunched-up look on his face. Then he turned to me and said, "You hear that?"

I hadn't heard a thing. I told him so.

He turned to Grant. "You?"

Whatever it was, Grant hadn't heard it either.

"Dang!" Jimmy exclaimed. "It was loud as day!"

Settling himself back down, he went on with his ice-fishing story. But he hadn't gotten very far before he stopped again and yelled, "There it is! They're talking to me!"

Once again, I had missed it. Grant, too.

The old fella swore beneath his breath. "I must be goin' crazy, just like they say!"

"Can you tell what the voices were saying?" I asked.

Jimmy frowned and shook his head from side to side. "Never can, really. I just know they're saying *something*."

He also turned on his clock radio and his television, saying the voices had come from them as well. We didn't hear a thing. That is, outside of what you would expect to hear from a clock radio and a TV.

This went on for hours. We learned what Jimmy thought of cable TV, which wasn't much, but we didn't hear any of the voices he had described. Finally, I took Grant aside and asked him what he thought. He shrugged. Jimmy had a problem—that much was evident. Whether it was of supernatural origin was difficult to say.

"I wish we could help this guy," I said.

"Me, too," said Grant. "But if we can't hear what he's hearing . . ."

"How do we know he's hearing it?"

Grant nodded. "Exactly."

A moment later, we heard Jimmy yelling for us. "Hurry up!" he shouted at the top of his lungs. "It's happening!"

We tracked him down to his bedroom. He was standing beside his clock radio, pointing to it. I listened, but all I heard was a news report.

Then I realized there was something else coming from the radio—another voice, underneath the newscaster's. It wasn't clear enough or loud enough for me to make out the words, but it was there. No question about it.

The voice went on for almost a minute, fading in and out. Then it stopped altogether, and again all I heard was the newscast. I turned to Grant and he gave me a look. Obviously, he had heard the voice, too.

So Jimmy was right. There *were* voices. But where were they coming from? Who or what was responsible for them?

As the night wore on, we didn't experience anything else. We also didn't get any clues to the source of the voices. After a while, Jimmy went to bed. It had been a long day for him. Grant and I, on the other hand, left our cameras and recorders running and went outside to think.

We put our backs against the wall of Jimmy's house and sat down on the ground. Then we considered everything we had seen, heard, or discussed since we arrived. The night sky was lit with a thousand stars. They stretched from the trees on one side of us to the houses on the other. I gazed aimlessly at the rooftops of Jimmy's neighbors, huddled together as if for warmth.

Suddenly, I realized what the problem was. "I've got it!" I said.

Grant looked at me. "What?"

I told him. Then I opened Jimmy's door, too eager to knock, and called for him. He came out of his room a moment later, his eyes shrunken with sleep. He must have decided to get some shuteye.

"I think I've got your answer," I told him.

I had noticed that his neighbor had a shortwave antenna on his roof. I recognized what it was because I had played around with CB radios when I was younger, and they used the same kind of antenna. It was designed to swing around so the guy who owned it could send his shortwave beams in different directions.

"I'll be damned," said Jimmy.

The next day, we called on his neighbor and confirmed that he had a shortwave radio set up in his basement, which he used at certain times of day when he could skip the signal over the oceans and get more distance out of it. The signal was bleeding into Jimmy's hearing aid, his television, his clock radio . . . pretty much anything designed to pick up a certain frequency.

Just to make sure I was on the money, we asked Jimmy's neighbor to turn on his radio. Then we sat down in Jimmy's bedroom, gathered around his clock radio, and turned it on. Sure enough, we could hear voices—the same ones Jimmy had been hearing for some time. Except they weren't from "the other side." They were from no farther than the house next door.

Once he realized what he was doing to Jimmy, the neighbor said he would curtail his shortwave usage. But Jimmy didn't mind it anymore. He was just happy to know what was going on. Grant and I were happy, too. We hadn't found any evidence of ghostly activity but we had helped Jimmy get to the bottom of his problem, and that was every bit as satisfying.

Jason: The Long Cleansing

2002

When Grant, three of our associates, and I drove up to the Borcher residence in our T.A.P.S. van, we saw a large, graceful, raised ranch-style home in a pleasant, snow-covered suburb of Fall River, Massachusetts.

The place had been built only ten years earlier, and it was still in mint condition. It wasn't exactly your typical den of supernatural activity. After all, paranormal activity is rare even in older houses, where a lot has taken place over the years. In a place that new, it was more likely that we would encounter a cranky pipe or an overactive imagination than an angry spirit.

But then, you never know.

Arthur and Phyllis Borcher were the house's original owners. Their younger daughter, Rachel, had lived there all her life. Their older daughter, Rebeccah, had moved in with them when she was just a toddler. Until recently, they had enjoyed living in their airy, tastefully decorated eight-room house.

Then the trouble started, or so the Borchers had told us over the phone. Their children had been attacked at night by something they couldn't see. Arthur heard Phyllis calling his name even when he was alone in their home, and vice versa. Strange lights appeared in one room or another, and then vanished when Arthur or Phyllis went to investigate. Shadows and what appeared to be human figures showed up in different parts of the house, faded, and showed up again somewhere else.

As always, a couple of us sat down with the homeowners while the rest looked around for places to set up our equipment. In this case, Grant and I spoke with the Borchers. They seemed defensive, as if they didn't quite trust us.

We understood how they felt. It's not easy to bring strangers into your home and give them the run of the place. And if people look at you funny every time you mention your experiences, you become reluctant to mention them any longer—even to the team of investigators you brought in to solve the problem.

We assured the Borchers that we were there to help, not to judge them. If their trouble stemmed from something paranormal, and we could document the activity, we would recommend certain actions. If it stemmed from something else, we hoped to be able to tell them that, too.

A quick walkthrough of the downstairs rooms, including the living room, the library, and the computer room, failed to yield any insights into the family's problems. There were no books in the home that had anything to do with the paranormal. The same was true of the Borchers' video collection. No hard-core horror films, no occult material, nothing you would call fear-based.

Whenever possible, we try to interview the various members of a household separately. That way their accounts are pure and unadulterated. There's no one there to influence them, to tell them what to say and what to withhold.

Also, if their stories don't match, you have to ask yourself why. We don't go into an investigation assuming that anyone is lying. Far from it, in fact. We have nothing but sympathy for anyone affected by the paranormal.

However, we have to take a scientific approach, which means maintaining a sense of skepticism and checking our facts every way we can. It's that skepticism that sets us apart from other ghost-hunting operations. Before we rely on a claim, we hold it up to the most intense scrutiny possible.

That's why I obtained permission to speak with seven-year-old Rachel in private. I asked her what kind of things had been happening in her house. She said that she had seen her older sister in bed at night moaning about not being able to get up, or about having a weight on her chest. At such times, she told us, she had seen what appeared to be a black shadow holding her sister down.

Rachel said that she herself had never been attacked by the black shadow, and that she had never had the feeling of a weight on top of her. However, she had felt her bed shaking at night, to the point that it felt like it was lifting off the ground. She had trouble going to sleep at night because of that, and also because she was worried that she, too, would be assaulted by the black shadow.

Next I spoke with Rebeccah, also in private. She hadn't heard my conversation with her younger sister, but she told me exactly the same story. She woke sometimes in the middle of the night to feel herself being held down by something heavy, something that looked black and shapeless. It made her afraid all the time, not just at night. I could see from the way her eyes moved around the room that she was extremely nervous, even with our T.A.P.S. team in the house.

Our interviews complete, Grant and I visited the second floor of the house. For one thing, we wanted to see how the equipment set-up was going. For another, we wanted to check out the sites where so much of the reported activity had taken place.

There were three bedrooms upstairs, two on the left side of the stairs and one on the right. The bedroom on the right was used as a storage room. It was full of boxes and children's toys, as well as odds and ends. There was also a bathroom up there, right at the top of the stairs.

Our exploration of the master bedroom turned up nothing of interest. The girls' bedroom seemed just as innocuous at first—until we discovered a Ouija board tucked all the way under the older girl's bed.

The attic was a small, unremarkable storage area. However, it was a lot hotter than the floors below it—thirty degrees hotter, according to our thermometers. If it had been July, we might not have been so concerned about the temperature differential, as attics are known for getting hot in the summertime. But this was February, right in the middle of winter. It was a red flag, to say the least.

At about four-thirty in the afternoon, we went back downstairs and sat down again with Arthur and Phyllis. In the meantime, the rest of our team continued setting up infrared cameras, laser thermometers, sound recorders, and other equipment to monitor activity in the home.

We told the Borchers that we had found a Ouija board under Rebeccah's bed, and that her use of this item could possibly have been the cause of the activity in the house.

With the Borchers' permission, we asked Rebeccah to join us. She came in kind of sheepishly, no doubt wondering what was going on. We asked her about the Ouija board, and whether she had used it.

She said that she had developed an interest in the board because her friends had told her she could use it to contact ghosts. She admitted to playing around with it three to four times a week, at night when her parents were asleep. She also conceded that her problems had started soon after she began using the board.

We explained to Rebeccah that we believed while Ouija boards can indeed contact spirits, they are too often the malicious kind. These spirits see their chance to invade our world and do so, often without the user of the board knowing what the spirit is doing.

Rebeccah seemed to understand. She promised us and her parents that she would get rid of the board and never use such a thing again.

As soon as we were done speaking with Rebeccah, we

called our team together for a meeting. We told them about the girl's use of the Ouija board and what we might be up against as a result. Everyone nodded.

At six-fifteen, just a few minutes after our meeting was over, the door to Rebeccah's bedroom slammed closed—apparently on its own. We checked to see if a window was open and had let in a breeze, but we couldn't find any such thing, or for that matter any other explanation. What's more, as we were pondering the incident, the door opened and slammed again. And it kept on opening and slamming, over and over again, for almost three minutes.

Naturally, we attempted to record the activity. But as soon as we brought a camcorder near the room, it died—even though its batteries had been charged just that morning, before we left Rhode Island. Our audio recorders wouldn't record anything either. When we played them back, we heard nothing but static.

After the door stopped slamming, it got quiet in the house. Grant and I agreed, however, that we would see more activity that night before we were done. As it turned out, we weren't disappointed.

At about eight o'clock, we heard a crashing noise come from the attic. We had placed a camcorder up there, so we were eager to see if it had picked up an image that would explain the noise. When we got there, we saw that the camcorder was no longer where we had left it. It had been pushed about fifteen feet across the dusty wooden floor and flipped over on its side.

When we played back the camcorder video, we saw what appeared to be a shadow moving in the attic. Then the picture slipped sideways, as if the camera had been struck from the right side and sent flying to its left. Fortunately, the camera didn't seem to have been damaged.

Again, nothing happened for a while. But with two incidents under our belt, we were willing to be patient. Around ten o'clock, our patience was rewarded. We heard voices in the upstairs hallway, as if someone were having a conversation up there, even though the family and our T.A.P.S. people were all downstairs. When we ascended the stairs to investigate, the voices went silent.

But something else was taking place in the house. The temperature rose about fifteen degrees in the span of just a few minutes. The air around us seemed to get thicker. And the noises we had heard were coming back, not just at the top of the stairs but all over the place.

At 10:30 P.M., we heard loud banging noises coming from the girls' room. When we went to investigate what was making the noises, we saw one of the beds shaking, just as Rachel had described. But it only went on for a moment. Then, as if whatever was moving it had registered our presence, it stopped.

At this time, we asked the Borchers what they thought about the possibility of cleansing the house through religious provocation. They were all for it. After all, they had been suffering for some time. They had been frustrated and frightened, and they wanted their daughters to be able to sleep in their own bedroom without having to worry about supernatural intruders.

One member of our T.A.P.S. team, Kevin, was a Catholic priest, and he was willing to perform the cleansing ritual. We decided, in concert with the Borchers, that he should bless the girls' room first. As he began to do so, we heard loud growls from what sounded like several different parts of the house.

I got the feeling that the growls were intended to distract us from what we were doing. Grant made the same observation. If so, the distraction didn't work. Despite the noises, we continued to cleanse the girls' bedroom.

By eleven o'clock, the ritual was complete and the growling stopped. However, we had addressed the problem in only one room. We had a lot more work to do.

At about half past eleven, Cole took advantage of the lull in activity to use the bathroom on the second floor. But no sooner had he crossed the threshold to the room than the door slammed shut in his face. Fortunately, he was able to get his hand up to ward off the blow, or his nose would certainly have been broken. We notified the rest of the team about Cole's experience and warned them to be alert for other kinds of dangerous activity.

As it turned out, I was the one involved in the next incident. As I was walking up the stairs, I felt myself struck by something from behind. I turned around to see what it was, but there was nothing there. And yet, a second later, something began pushing me up the stairs. I resisted, and the force got progressively weaker. After nearly a minute or so, it went away altogether.

But it had driven home a point in my mind: It was unsafe for any of us to go it alone anywhere in the house. Whatever had come to inhabit the Borcher house seemed to feel threatened by our presence, and might attack a lone investigator.

Meanwhile, Kevin was continuing to bless one part of the residence after another. By twelve-thirty, we began to hear loud noises again, banging and slamming from those parts of the house that had not yet been blessed. Since the living room had already been cleansed, we felt comfortable leaving the family in that room.

At 1:05 A.M., the noises stopped again. Grant and I wondered why, since the cleansing ritual was still going on. He suggested that the entity might be trying to gather its strength for another kind of attack.

At one-fifteen, Ed and Cole went into the kitchen to make themselves something to eat. But as soon as they entered the room, they were confronted by the sight of the kitchen chairs sliding at them across the floor. Fortunately, the chairs stopped when they reached the doorway to the kitchen.

Ed and Cole came to see us immediately. They told us what they had seen, and assured us that they could wait until later to eat something. Apparently, they preferred to sit on chairs that stayed where they were.

By one-forty-five, we had blessed six out of the eight rooms in the house. As we continued to work, we recommended that the family stay together in the living room, just in case. Also, we made sure that there were always two members of our team with them at all times.

By two-fifteen, the place had been quiet for about an hour, and we were starting to wonder if the entity was still present. Either way, we were going to finish blessing the house. After all, there were only two parts of it we hadn't yet covered—the attic and the ground-floor library.

At three in the morning, the silence was broken by crashing sounds coming from the library. When Ed and Cole went to investigate, they saw that dozens of books had been torn from the library's built-in shelves and thrown all over the room. As they picked up the books, they asked for permission to set up camp in the library. Grant and I gave them the go-ahead, so that they could witness anything else that might take place there.

At about 3:30 A.M., Grant and I went up to the attic to see if there had been additional activity there as well. Almost as soon as we arrived, we were visited by a large dark mass. Usually, such things linger only for a moment and then depart. This one floated about the attic as if in defiance of our presence there.

Finally, after a couple of minutes, the thing appeared to melt its way through the floor. Instantly, the two-way radios we had been using started to go haywire, keeping us from communicating with our associates downstairs. Grant and I descended from the attic to see if the mass might appear again somewhere else.

Sure enough, we heard from Ed and Cole a moment later, our two-way radios suddenly working fine again. "There's something down here in the library," Ed told us, his voice hushed in awe. "Something big and black."

Grant looked at me. "We'll be right there," he said.

We reached the library just in time to see the black mass vanish through the south wall of the room. Grant and I were concerned that it would appear somewhere else, so we kept looking through the house. But that was the last we would see of it.

At approximately four o'clock in the morning, we began to bless the attic. At that point, Grant was staying with the family, who—in their exhaustion—had all gone to sleep in Arthur and Phyllis's room.

Up in the attic, we heard howling noises coming from

somewhere below us. Later on, Grant told me that he could hear them as well, and that they seemed to be coming from the library. After a while, the family woke up, alarmed by the noises. The girls were hysterical, Rachel in particular.

Grant told them that such activity wasn't unexpected. Spirits didn't like to be evicted from a place in which they had gotten comfortable. This one was howling in the hope of disrupting the cleansing. However, its howling would last only until the priest was finished with the ritual.

The girls were fearful that the entity would come after them in their parents' bedroom. Grant explained that they were safe there. The entity could only enter one room of the house now, and that was the library, because every other room had already been closed to it through the priest's blessing.

By four-thirty we were all bone-tired, but the library was still a haven for the entity. We couldn't let it remain that way. Taking a deep breath, the priest started to bless the library as he had blessed the rest of the house. Again, books started flinging themselves off the shelves, striking the priest and the other members of our team. Loud screams could be heard throughout the house.

Then, abruptly, it all stopped—the books, the noises, and the feeling of chaos. We looked at each other. The priest composed himself and said to the entity, as was customary at such times, "Give us a sign of your departure."

Suddenly, the bookshelf on the north wall of the library fell over and crashed against the floor, spilling its contents. We had received a sign, all right, and a dramatic one. The battle was over, and we had won.

After that, the air in the house had a new feel to it. It

wasn't stifling anymore. At five in the morning, we finally went to sleep—not just the family, but our team as well. It was a well-deserved rest, if a brief one.

By 8:00 A.M. we were up again, packing our equipment and loading it into our van. In the light of morning, it's always hard to believe the events of the night before. This instance was no exception.

But what a night it had been. We had seen the dark mass manifest on more than one occasion, and in more than one part of the house. We had heard the growling that seemed to take place in protest of our cleansing ritual. We had seen Rachel's bed shake, if only for a moment. Doors had slammed, one of them in Cole's face. Our camcorder appeared to have been thrown across the attic. I was shoved up the stairs by something I couldn't see. We recorded a temperature spike, chairs slid across the kitchen floor, and books flew off the library shelves—not just once, but twice.

Some night, all right. But it seemed to have ended well. We were wrung out, spent. But we had accomplished something meaningful on behalf of the Borchers, so the effort was well worth it.

Before we left, we confiscated Rebeccah's Ouija board. We also made sure the family had our number in case we had missed something. Religious provocation isn't a science, after all. It's not foolproof.

But we have spoken with Arthur and Phyllis several times over the years since our investigation, and they haven't experienced any further problems. Their home is calm, peaceful. They're living the life they hoped to live, free of the entity that had caused them so much pain.

GHOST HUNTER'S MANUAL: THE TEAM

A paranormal investigation is only as good as the team you bring to it. The right chemistry can make for an easy night, and a very productive one. The wrong chemistry can turn a ghost hunt into a . . . well, a nightmare.

First off, you need a chain of command. It sounds great to say that everyone's going to be an equal partner in the investigation, but ghost-hunting doesn't lend itself to democracy. It's a field where hundreds of decisions have to be made on the fly, and there's seldom time for a discussion among equals.

That's why there's got to be one person in charge at any given time. Maybe it's not the same person every night. Maybe you want to rotate the top spot every so often. But we can tell you there's one person in every group who's better equipped for leadership than any of the others, and if you're smart, that's the person you'll eventually defer to on a regular basis.

Of course, you won't be able to ask that person for advice at every turn. Sometimes there's just no time for communication. You may have to move quickly or take a chance on losing a valuable piece of evidence. But what might seem like an emergency to one person might not seem that way to another.

That's when things start to fall apart. You've got the guy in charge saying the investigator should have deferred to him, and the investigator insisting that there wasn't enough time to do so, and everyone else standing around and rolling their eyes. Both parties in the controversy think they're right, and you'll never convince either one of them to change his mind.

Our advice is to establish a system of protocols at the outset. Make it clear what everyone's responsibility is in any given instance. For example, who's going to set up the cameras? Who's going to interview the client? It's embarrassing and unprofessional to make those decisions in front of the people you're trying to help—the people who should have confidence in your ability to carry out an investigation.

Your system of protocols should also tell you which actions require clearance from the lead investigator and which can be initiated by just about anyone. You don't want to tie anyone's hands and keep him from making an important discovery, but you also don't want everyone going off and doing his own thing. That way lies chaos, not to mention bickering, personal danger, and the possibility that your investigation will be a serious waste of time.

Which makes it all the more important to have the right people on the job in the first place. If you pick good personnel, they'll understand the need for both protocols and a chain of command, and they'll find ways to make important and even unexpected contributions within the bounds of their job descriptions. It's even better if each of them brings a particular expertise to the party—say, a knack for working with electronics, or a sensitivity to the presence of the supernatural, or just a talent for packing and unpacking the equipment van.

More than anything, you need people with patience. If ghost-hunting is about anything, it's about remaining vigilant—watching and listening and taking careful notes. Personal experiences with the paranormal are rare. You can't afford to miss one because your concentration slipped for just a moment.

It's also helpful if the members of your team get along with one another. After all, they're going to be spending a lot of long hours sitting next to one another in some dark place. If they enjoy one another's company, it makes for a smoother and infinitely more entertaining investigation.

Lord knows we've seen the other kind. Guys getting on each other's nerves, goofing off and forcing other people to pick up the slack, making silly mistakes that undo a lot of hard work. Yeah, we've seen it, and it isn't pretty.

One of the reasons the two of us have worked together as long as we have is that we like each other. If we weren't hunting ghosts together, we would be doing something else. In fact, we often *are* doing something else.

Not that friendship is always a guarantee that you'll work well together. In fact, we've seen friendships come crashing to a halt because two guys get on each other's nerves in the course of an investigation. The important thing isn't whether you're friends when you go into a client's house.

It's whether you're friends when you come out.

Grant: Protector

2002

Most of the time, people contact us in an attempt to prove once and for all whether they've got ghosts in their house. In those cases, we bring in our team and do our best to document anything that might be going on. And, of course, our clients wait eagerly to find out what we've discovered, if anything.

But sometimes, a client isn't looking for validation. He just wants some insight, some advice based on the expertise we've gained over the years. When that happens, we're more than willing.

Especially when the welfare of a teenaged girl is at stake.

Back in the winter of 2002, we were contacted by the Barnetts, an upper-middle-class family of four in eastern Rhode Island. Jim and Lydia Barnett had two daughters, twenty-year-old Cynthia and eighteen-year-old Dara. They were all nice people, very sweet, very hospitable, and from all outward indications very happy.

From what they told us, they had been experiencing paranormal activity in their house since Dara was ten years old. However, it was very benign activity. The family had a feeling that there was someone there with them, comforting them and helping them out in little ways.

Their guest, whatever it was, seemed to have a particular affinity for Dara. Items that she lost would turn up in obvious places, doors would open for her, and lights would turn on for her. The idea that a spirit in the house was looking out for her didn't frighten her in the least. In fact, it was a source of great delight to her.

At the point when the family called us in, Dara had a boyfriend named Jeffrey. At first, the Barnetts had embraced him. After all, he seemed like a perfect gentleman, just the sort of young man they wanted their daughter to be seeing. Then Jeffrey began to show his true colors.

It showed first in the way he talked to Dara, which was increasingly impatient and eventually downright rude. Then he became physically abusive, grabbing her by the wrist and pushing her around. There was no telling what he would do next.

Finally he became bolder and began abusing Dara within the confines of her house. Then, out of nowhere, an unseen force began to intervene. The first time Jeffrey tried to grab Dara in her kitchen, he was pushed out of the room and had the door swing closed behind him.

Another time he went after Dara in a fit of rage and was tripped before he could get to her. On a third occasion, he was angry with her and chased her up to her room, where the door slammed shut in his face and locked itself. Dara cringed inside the room, listening to her boyfriend shouting incoherently and banging on the door.

Suddenly, he fell silent. After a while, Dara opened the door and saw that Jeffrey was calm again. And pale, as if something had scared the daylights out of him. Later on, when she asked Jeffrey about what happened, he refused to talk about it.

When Dara saw what was happening to Jeffrey, she became concerned. After all, if he could be attacked in her house, someone else could be handled that way as well. She worried about her girlfriends, her family, and even herself.

We explained to Dara that, while we couldn't say for sure until we conducted an investigation, it seemed she was being protected by a spirit in the house. We told her and her parents—who were shocked to hear about Jeffrey's behavior—that it was in their best interest to validate the entity's existence. But either way, it was doing Dara a favor, so it would be best to let it stay.

We also suggested to Dara that she get a new boyfriend. Maybe it wasn't our place to do so, but teenagers are often more likely to listen to an outsider than to their own parents. In any case, she broke up with Jeffrey.

Since that time, no one else in the house has been attacked.

Jason:
Bad Advice

2003

Elizabeth Mitchell was hearing voices.

A sixty-three-year-old woman, she lived alone in her house in Eaton, Connecticut. She had never shown any signs of being delusional or mentally unstable. As far as anyone could tell, she had always been a good mother, a good wife, and a good citizen.

But the voices were telling her to do things she didn't think were right. Bad things. Hurtful things. The voices wanted her to do these things not only to her next-door neighbor, with whom Elizabeth had always gotten along, but also to her thirty-six-year-old daughter, Kaitlyn, who would visit the house every so often.

Elizabeth didn't want to do these things. But if she didn't, the voices would hurt her. They told her so. So she did what the voices said.

She took her garbage out and, instead of taking it to the curb, threw it over the fence into her neighbor's yard. Naturally, her neighbor was upset when she found Elizabeth's garbage in her flowerbed. But Elizabeth was too frightened of the voices not to do it again and again, as often as they asked.

When Kaitlyn dropped by, she expected that her mother would be the same loving woman who had raised her. But that wasn't what she found. After all, the voices were telling Elizabeth to be mean to her daughter, and to say to her that she wasn't welcome anymore in the house.

After a while, Kaitlyn stopped coming over so often. And as her mother's treatment of her grew worse and worse, she stopped coming at all. At the voices' insistence, Elizabeth had destroyed the most important relationship she had in the entire world.

But they didn't stop there. They told Elizabeth to act mean to everyone, friends, relatives, and acquaintances alike. One by one, Elizabeth alienated them all with her behavior. Finally, she had no one to talk to but the voices.

It was at that point, in the spring of 2003, after she had destroyed the last of her relationships with the people she loved, that she contacted T.A.P.S. Elizabeth told us about the voices, and that she was afraid they belonged to demons. She wanted very much to get rid of them, and hoped we could help her.

We brought in a team of investigators, set up our equipment, and spent the night checking out her house. However, we couldn't come up with any evidence to indicate that Elizabeth was experiencing something paranormal.

None of us saw or heard anything that would lead us in that direction.

Afterward, when we returned to Warwick, we reviewed our data. Sometimes a seemingly uneventful investigation turns out to be chock full of suspicious video images and EVPs. But that wasn't true of Elizabeth's case. We didn't come up with anything we could call evidence.

Jason and I returned to Eaton and explained our findings to her. She was disappointed, to say the least. She had hoped that we could help her with her problem, and now she wondered if there was any hope for her.

However, we did have a suggestion for her. We referred her to a friend of ours who is a clinical psychiatrist. Since we had already tried the paranormal approach without success, we believed Elizabeth should explore the medical angle.

Our friend examined her and found that she was schizophrenic. He prescribed medication for her condition, and over time she began to see an improvement. The voices went away . . . and they haven't come back since.

Grant: The Littlest Sleepwalker

2003

If you watch *Ghost Hunters* on Syfy, you know that Jason and I are plumbers. More specifically, you know that we're plumbers for Roto-Rooter, the sewer- and drain-cleaning operation that everyone has used at least once in his life, or so it seems.

I used to be in the computer business, way back when. Jason too. But after a while, he left it to work as a plumber at Roto-Rooter, and eventually he asked me to work with him there. I agreed, and I've never looked back.

What do I like about plumbing? Well, for one thing, I get to solve problems. I've always enjoyed that. For another thing, I get to use my hands. I've always enjoyed that as well. Finally, I get to work with Jason.

Well, two out of three ain't bad.

Sorry, I couldn't resist. The truth is that working with

Jay is a great bonus. While we're installing a water heater or pulling out a sink, we have an opportunity to talk. We discuss the paranormal investigation we just finished, the one we're in the middle of, or maybe the one we're about to start. We talk about our team, our equipment, and our approaches to certain situations.

An expertise in plumbing has been a big help to us in our ghost-hunting work. We've learned enough about the trade, and home construction in general, to be able to debunk a lot of the claims made by our clients. They can rest easier knowing their problem is a noisy pipe and not a supernatural entity trying to get their attention.

Once in a while, plumbing is helpful in another way. It enables us to run into paranormal phenomena we would never have encountered otherwise. Take, for example, the case of Debbie and Ellie Johnson, who called Roto-Rooter to their southern Rhode Island home about six years ago.

Jason and I answered the call. The problem, we could see immediately, was the main line stack. We were down in the Johnsons' basement, repairing it, when we were joined by five-year-old Ellie, one of the cutest kids you've ever seen.

She didn't come too close, but she was clearly interested in watching us work. Jay and I love kids so, of course, we said and did some things designed to make her laugh. We were successful, too.

After a while Ellie went back upstairs, and her mother joined us in the basement instead. She chatted with us as we worked, and somehow the subject of our other line of work—paranormal investigation—came up. Debbie was intrigued and looked as if she wanted to tell us something, but was afraid to say it. After some curious, gentle prodding on our parts, she finally found the courage.

"It's been going on for a while now," she said.

"What has?" I asked.

"Ellie's sleepwalking. The first time I woke up and realized she wasn't in her room, I flew into a panic. I found her walking around in the yard, the back door wide open. I picked her up and put her back in bed, and assured myself that it was an isolated incident. I told myself it would never happen again."

But it did. Of course, Ellie didn't always wind up in the yard—especially after Debbie placed a lock on the back door too high for her daughter to reach. Sometimes Ellie wound up in the kitchen, or in the living room, or in the basement.

When Debbie corraled her, she asked her where she was going—not loudly or abruptly, but softly. After all, she had heard something about it being bad to wake a sleepwalker. Ellie always answered the same way, referring to "a girl" and "being in old times."

Debbie was at her wits' end. She had spoken to their family doctor, but none of his suggestions seemed to have worked. Jason and I told her that we would like to come back and help her out.

She said she couldn't afford to pay us much. "We don't ask for money," I told her. "We just like to do whatever we can."

We conducted three investigations of the Johnson house, which turned out to be even older than it looked. Along the way, we captured a handful of EVPs. Each of them sounded like the voice of a little girl, but none of them had come from Ellie. They belonged to someone else—someone unseen.

It wasn't until our fourth visit that we caught Ellie sleepwalking. Her eyes were open, but they had a distant look to them. As we watched, she went to the house's back door and stood there, staring outside.

We recommended to Debbie that we let her daughter out of the house and follow her. For a moment, she looked as if she didn't know what to do. Then she unlocked the door that led to the yard.

Walking on small, bare feet, Ellie led us through the quiet, moonlit woods. She had never been out this way before, according to her mother, but she seemed to know exactly where she was going. Eventually, she stopped and looked out into the darkness between the trees.

At first, we couldn't see anything out there. Then we picked out what looked like headstones, though they were small and rounded off by the elements. It looked like an old, forgotten family cemetery.

When we said so, Debbie's hands went up to her face. She couldn't believe what we had found. Neither she nor any of her neighbors had known the cemetery was there, just a couple of hundred yards from her property.

In the dark, it was hard to tell what was carved on the stones. We told Debbie that we would come back after dawn and take another look. She nodded. Then she picked up her daughter and carried her back to the house.

In the morning, Jay and I did as we promised. We found several stones, a few of them so sunken into the ground that we would have missed them if we hadn't caught sight of the others. When we scraped away the vines and the debris, we were able to read the names carved into their surfaces.

Our next stop was Town Hall. We were able to find the family name we had seen on the stones without any problem, and also the fact that a cemetery was located behind what was now Debbie's property. However, there was no information on the individuals who were buried there.

It wouldn't have been an urgent matter if one of them wasn't still around in spirit, making its presence felt in Ellie's life. For that reason alone we had to do something. But even if the little girl wasn't affected, Jay and I would still have tried to ease the entity's discomfort.

We discussed the matter with Debbie and she agreed that we should put a marker there acknowledging the people buried in those forgotten graves. Once we did that, Ellie stopped sleepwalking.

Jason:
The Frying Pan

2003

Annie Dinkins had a problem.

On the phone, she sounded like a sweet little old lady, the kind you might meet at a bake sale. Unlike most of our clients, she didn't sound scared—maybe a little concerned, but definitely not scared. She told us that she was hearing voices in her house and hadn't been able to find their source. Without any other explanation to fall back on, she had come to the conclusion that the place was haunted.

We acknowledged that she might be experiencing supernatural activity, but we wouldn't be able to say for certain until we conducted an investigation. She thought that was a good idea. We told her that we would come by as soon as possible.

After all, she might have been sitting on a bigger problem

than she realized. The fact that she wasn't frightened didn't mean she didn't have *reason* to be frightened. Packing up our equipment, we got out to her place before the light died.

When we arrived, we made a circuit around the house. It didn't look at all unusual. But then, we had learned from long experience that appearances could be deceiving. Ringing the doorbell, we waited to meet our client.

Annie was every bit the sweet little old lady she had seemed to be on the phone. She led us into the living room, where all the furniture was covered in plastic, and told us to sit down while she brought in some cookies. We told her that she didn't have to go to any trouble, but she insisted. While we were waiting, a couple of cats slunk into the room and deposited themselves in our laps.

Just then, Annie came in with a tray full of milk and cookies. We thanked her and tried to begin our interview, but she said she wouldn't think of speaking with us until we'd sampled some of the treats she had brought us.

Touched by Annie's hospitality, we had a couple of cookies apiece and washed them down with the milk. Finally, we asked her to repeat her story and include everything she could think of. As she complied, she took the plate of cookies off the tray and put it on the coffee table in front of us. Then she took the tray and our glasses back into the kitchen, making it difficult for us to hear what she was saying.

I glanced at Grant. He smiled and shrugged. Obviously, we were going to have to wait until Annie returned to the living room to make any sense of her story.

A minute later, Annie rejoined us. But she was no longer the sweet little old lady who had plied us with milk and cookies. She looked mad as hell, her face red and pinched, and as she screamed at us we noticed that she had a frying pan in her hand.

Suddenly, she launched herself across the room at us. Flinging the cats out of our laps, Grant and I scattered. Fortunately, we were a little faster than our host, or we would have had a couple of dents in our skulls.

"Hang on!" I said, retreating behind the couch and holding up my hands for peace. "Please, try to calm down!"

But she kept after us, wielding the frying pan and telling us to get out of her house while we still could. Clearly, she had no recollection at all of having invited us into her living room or serving us cookies. As far as she was concerned we were intruders, and she was determined to show us she was no easy target.

We reminded her of who we were and why we were there. Not once, but repeatedly. Finally, she relented. Then, as it all came back to her, she apologized profusely. She even had tears in her eyes.

Annie wasn't the victim of supernatural entities. Sad to say, she was the victim of dementia. It was a pity, too. She was the nicest little old lady you can imagine—when she didn't have a frying pan in her hand.

Grant: The Priest

2003

Frank and Linda Bolton, residents of a small town in western Connecticut, lived in a house next door to a Catholic church. They had liked the location when they first saw it because it made them feel secure, even though they weren't Catholics themselves.

But shortly after they moved in, their feelings of security faded. There was something going on in their house, something strange and alarming. Though they had never believed in ghosts before, their experiences were leading them to the inescapable conclusion that their home was haunted.

First Frank and Linda heard organ music, a lot like what was played at the church next door. However, they heard it in the middle of the night, long after the church had shut its doors. So where, they wondered, was it coming from?

Then they began finding religious artifacts around the house—crucifixes and rosaries they had never seen before in their lives. They wondered if someone was playing a joke on them. If so, they weren't laughing.

And it got worse. They started seeing a tall, thin figure in different parts of the house, a figure that seemed to be looking for something. Whenever they stared at it long enough, it disappeared. But the sight stayed with them, and scared them so much they wanted to leave the house.

One morning, Linda took a shower and saw something scrawled in the steamy surface of her bathroom mirror. Looking more closely, she saw that it was the word "whore." Frank didn't know how it had gotten there. In fact, he was every bit as shaken up as Linda was.

The last straw was when the couple was making love in their bedroom, and they saw a figure sitting on the floor. It seemed to be watching them, without making a sound. Yet when Frank flipped on the lights, there was no one there.

The next morning, he contacted T.A.P.S.

His claims were disturbing, even to us. More important, they were potentially dangerous, so we dropped everything and drove down to see the Boltons. We told them that we would try to capture what they had seen and heard, and either corroborate their claims or find explanations for them.

Setting up our equipment, we waited to see what would happen. We only had one experience the entire night—a glimpse of a shadowy figure that might have been the apparition the Boltons were talking about. But it was hard to tell.

Frank and Linda were disappointed when we told them that a shadow was all we had seen. However, we had a fair amount of data to go over. We allowed for the possibility that something more substantial would turn up in our recordings.

Back home, we went over our audiotapes as carefully as we could in the hope of hearing some EVPs. As it turned out, we caught only one. However, it was very clear and distinct—the name "Leonard."

And that wasn't all. The camera we had placed in the Boltons' upstairs hallway had caught a tall, shadowy figure. As Jay and I watched the tape, it walked into view, proceeded down the hallway in the direction of the camera, and faded away just before it reached the lens.

I sat back, impressed with the footage, and said, "Wow."

"Looks like we've got something to show the Boltons," said Jay. "And let's not forget that EVP. I wonder who Leonard is."

So did I. But we weren't going to find out sitting there in Jay's basement in Warwick, Rhode Island. As soon as we could, we went back to Connecticut in search of the man addressed in the EVP.

Researching the history of the Boltons' house, we discovered that several priests had lived in it over the years. One of them, it seemed, was a tall, gaunt fellow named Leonard. What's more, he departed the priesthood under mysterious circumstances. After ten years of service to the Church, he suddenly left for parts unknown—though no one we spoke to seemed to know why.

Was Leonard's spirit the one haunting the Boltons? He was tall and thin, like the apparition they had seen. But it seemed strange that a priest would use profanity, or intrude on the relations of a married couple.

We continued to investigate the house, looking for additional data. In the course of our efforts, one of our investigators realized she was missing a crucifix she always wore on a chain around her neck. Soon afterward, we found it lying in the bathroom—right under the mirror on which the Boltons had seen the word "whore."

Had the spirit in the house removed the crucifix from our investigator's chain? Why would it do such a thing? Did it think our investigator wasn't worthy of wearing a symbol of Christian holiness?

Maybe it had a similar view of Linda, though we couldn't find anything unsavory about the Boltons' behavior. Had the spirit been harassing them during sex because it thought they were engaged in something immoral? And was the spirit indeed that of Leonard, the priest who had left the order?

We had lots of questions. What we needed were some more answers. We decided it was time to speak to the priests at the church.

None of them was eager to speak about their former colleague. In fact, the very mention of his name made them uncomfortable. However, after we told them it was a matter of some importance, they confided in us that Leonard had been guilty of a sin—specifically, that of promiscuity. In fact, he had frequented certain houses of ill repute for some time. Finally, mounting pressure from his superiors in the Church and his own guilt compelled him to leave the priesthood.

That explained why his spirit had lingered in the house, and why it had interfered with the Boltons. It couldn't get over the sins it had committed, made worse by the fact that it was a priest who committed them. As a result, it saw what was perfectly normal human activity through the lens of its own guilt, and acted accordingly.

One of the priests at the church agreed to accompany us to the Boltons' house and speak with Leonard's spirit. Calmly and in a tone full of understanding, he explained to it that its sins were forgiven. There was no reason to stand guard over the house it had lived in, or to linger in this world. It could move on.

After that, the activity ceased. The Boltons never heard the eerie music again, found their bathroom mirror scrawled on, or had their intimate relations interrupted by a tall, disapproving apparition.

GHOST HUNTER'S MANUAL: RESEARCH 101

Okay. You've conducted your investigation. You've gotten lucky and had a couple of personal experiences that strongly suggest paranormal activity. Maybe you've even captured a few spine-chilling EVPs.

So you're pretty convinced that the place you investigated contains human spirits—the remains of people who lived or died on the site. And because you've done your job, starting with your client interviews, you know how these spirits behave. You know where they tend to show up, and what they do afterward.

But you probably don't know who they are or why they're tied to this venue. Or maybe you have a suspicion, but that's about it. And for your client's sake as well as your own, you'd love to be able to find out for sure.

That's where research comes in.

As we noted earlier, you don't want to conduct research in advance of your investigation because it'll skew the way you approach your client's claims. But now that you've collected and reviewed all your data, you don't have to worry anymore about being unduly influenced.

So where do you start?

How about with people? That is, the kind who are still breathing, brushing their teeth, and going to work in the morning. Ghost hunters spend so much time looking for the dead that they sometimes forget about the living. However, the elderly gent on the park bench across the street may know *exactly* why some spirit is crying out for help, or revenge, or whatever is keeping it from crossing over. After all, the guy has been around a while and remembers everything that went on.

Of course, there may be witnesses to a spirit's trauma who aren't very old at all. If the event in question took place just a few years ago, even a child may be aware of it. The key is to ask around, and then ask around some more. Eventually, you may find someone who says, "Sure I know what happened in that house. I was standing right there on the sidewalk when the ambulance came to pick her up . . ."

Then you know you're on to something.

On the other hand, you may not find anyone who can help you. Or maybe they fill in some of the blanks but not all of them. In either case, your next research stop should be Town Hall.

If you're an aspiring ghost hunter, you need to know that town halls are treasure troves of information. They have records that can tell you when a place was built, by whom, and what, if anything, stood there before. They can tell you who owned the place originally, whom they sold it to, who added on a whole new wing fifty years later, and who owns it now.

They also have vital records. They can tell you who was born in town and when. They can tell you who got married and who got divorced, along with all the pertinent dates. They can tell you who died, at what age, and under what circumstances.

Another good place to do research is the local library. If the event that's tying a spirit to a place is public knowledge, there may have been newspaper coverage of it. And libraries often keep old newspapers on microfiche, which you can scroll through in search of additional information.

This can be tedious work, no question about it. And you may walk out empty-handed. But you owe it to your client to get as much information as possible, and that means leaving no stone unturned.

Finally, you can visit the offices of the local historical society. Not every town has one, and not every society has a lot of reliable information, but some have more than you might think. If the people you're interested in were prominent citizens, there may be a stack of photos showing them at various town functions.

Our advice is to give the historical society a shot. Maybe you'll find someone who hasn't seen a visitor in weeks, and who can't wait to look up the information you need. In this business, you need all the help you can get.

So how does this all come together? After you've spoken with people in town, and then visited Town Hall, the library, and the historical society . . . what have you got? Maybe an awful lot.

Let's say you captured an EVP in the course of your investigation, and it sounds like someone calling for "Belle." You ask around and you find out from the elderly fellow next door that there was a Beverly Johnson who lived in the house you were investigating, but that everyone knew her as "Belle." Also, the neighbor tells you, Beverly died young—but he doesn't remember how.

At Town Hall, you look up the address of the house you're investigating. You see that a family named Johnson lived there all right, back in the 1930s and 1940s. Then you look up Beverly Johnson, and find that she died in childbirth.

When you visit the library, you discover that Belle Johnson's husband, John, was active in town government. In fact, there's a picture of him and his wife taken during an Easter Parade. It seems from the picture that the Johnsons were very much in love.

At the historical society, you find out that after Belle's death, John put their house up for sale. Then he and his newborn child moved to Boston to live with his sister's family. However, judging from the letters he sent back to his old neighbors, which were preserved by the society, he spent the rest of his life pining for his wife.

And if he missed her so in life, might he not continue to miss her after he was dead? It would certainly make sense. So it could be John's spirit calling out for his beloved Belle that was recorded as an EVP.

Now you've got the part of the story you couldn't get from a simple investigation. Which means you've also got something to talk about if your client wants to make contact with the spirit you discovered. And all of it was public information, available to anyone who bothered to look for it.

Grant: The Face in the Window—

2003

In the late fall, we got a call from a man named Alex Billingsley who lived in southern New Hampshire. He said that he and his family had seen some odd things in and around their house and were afraid that they were supernatural in origin.

They lived in a secluded location, in the middle of the woods. It seemed calm there, peaceful, easy on the nerves. But for the Billingsleys, the place had become something out of a dark and very disturbing nightmare.

They heard banging noises in the middle of the night. They had bad dreams. Objects, and sometimes also what appeared to be child-sized figures, had been seen flitting from room to room. More than once, they had caught glimpses of lights in the sky over their house.

The Billingsleys were clearly distraught about these

events and wanted to know what was happening to them. We told them we would do whatever we could to help. As soon as we could, Jason and I made the trip up to New Hampshire.

On our arrival, we talked extensively with Alex and his family and found them to be very down-to-earth people. They had even done some debunking of their own before calling us, finding natural explanations for some of the things they were experiencing. But they couldn't explain all of it.

We carried out a couple investigations at the Billingsleys' house with nothing more than a few unexplained sounds to show for our efforts. Alex assured us that there was a lot more to be found, and we remained determined to find it. On the night of the third investigation, we set up our equipment and waited as we had before.

Partway through the night, we heard scrabbling noises along the outside of the house. We went to check them out and failed to find anything. Still, neither Jason nor I had any doubt that we had heard them.

As we were pondering the cause of the sounds, we heard something else—what sounded like windows slamming up and down. Again, we couldn't identify the cause. Then we heard the scrape of footsteps.

Before we could investigate them, we heard a scream from one of the bedrooms. It turned out that one of the Billingsleys' daughters had started awake from what she described as a terrible nightmare. When we asked her about it, she didn't want to talk. She just pressed her face into her pillow and cried.

The rest of the night was uneventful. However, we had heard so many strange sounds that we were sure there was something going on. The daughter's experience was just the icing on the cake.

The next day, we reviewed the video and audio evidence—and were shocked by what we had recorded. On one camera, which was located in the living room, we saw a shadowy figure rise up from the bottom of one of the window frames and peer inside the home. As if that wasn't odd enough, the face and head of the figure, with its big, dark eyes, looked like something we had seen before . . . a gray alien.

In our experience, spirits didn't give that kind of appearance. They had the proportions of the people they had been before they died. And the lights seen by the family didn't fit into any ghostly patterns we had detected in the past.

So we had to at least entertain the possibility that we were dealing with an alien, or maybe several of them. It was difficult to say.

Now, extraterrestrials weren't exactly our area of expertise. We didn't know how to proceed, or even how to break this news to the family. Just to make sure, we conducted two more investigations. The results were much the same. In one case, we could clearly see a slender, humanlike figure walk by a set of sliding glass doors. The sounds, too, were similar to those we had heard earlier.

Finally, we contacted a friend of ours who does what we do except with aliens instead of supernatural entities. We convinced the Billingleys that it would be a good idea to speak with him. As we looked on, he sat in their living room and explained to the family that, based on the evidence we had gathered, there was a good chance they were the subject of scrutiny by extraterrestrials.

At first, the family was skeptical. However, as they considered everything that had happened to them, they realized that our friend might have the explanation they were looking for. He is working with the Billingsleys to this day, trying to make sense of their continuing experiences.

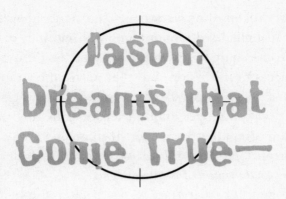

Dreams that Come True—

2003

D ierdre Perkins, a forty-year-old woman who lived in south central Massachusetts, had always been an optimist at heart. She had been the kind of person who liked to hike and canoe and take long bicycle trips, who got up every morning and went to work—which, in her case, meant managing a local warehouse—with a smile on her face.

But she wasn't that kind of person when Grant and I spoke to her on a dismal day in midwinter. By then, Dierdre was scared half to death, afraid to put her head down on the pillow because of the dreams she kept having.

"They're not normal dreams," she told us over the phone with a noticeable tightness in her voice. "Not normal at all."

"What do you mean?" I asked her.

In her dreams, she said, she was experiencing paranormal activity. It night be doors opening and closing, or strange sounds somewhere in the house, or shadows flitting around at the edges of her vision. But that wasn't the strange part. After all, a lot of people had dreams like those.

What was different about Dierdre's dreams was what happened after they were over. It might be a day later or a week later, but she would experience in real life *the exact same activity that she had dreamed about.*

We asked her to contact us again after she had one of those dreams, and we would be there to see if the activity really took place. Then, maybe, we could figure out what was going on. Dierdre agreed.

Weeks passed and we didn't hear from her. She finally called and told us she had a dream that the contents of her kitchen drawers were rattling and then three drawers opened and slammed shut. What's more, in the dream, Grant and I were present in the kitchen when it happened.

We looked at each other when she told us that. The perverse side of me wondered what would happen if we didn't show up. Would the drawers still open and close? Would anything take place at all?

Of course, we couldn't stay home when the possibility of recording paranormal activity beckoned. Also, we had made a commitment to Dierdre. It wouldn't be right to let her face her dream-come-true alone.

As soon as we could, we packed up our equipment and made the trip to Massachusetts. Dierdre was waiting for us outside the house when we got there. Obviously, she didn't want to face that kind of activity without company. Grant and I set up cameras and audio recorders all over the kitchen, trying to catch every angle possible, then hunkered down to see what would happen.

We waited for the better part of a day with no results. Day turned to night. Night turned back to day again. Diedre had said that it sometimes took a week for her dream to become reality. We had jobs, so we didn't have the option of staying there indefinitely. Fortunately, we didn't have to.

Deep into the second night of our vigil, the kitchen started to come alive with paranormal activity. Just as in Dierdre's dream, it started with a rattling sound, as if someone were trying to open the wooden drawers beneath the counters. Then, suddenly, three of the drawers opened almost at the same time and slammed shut again.

And we caught it all with our video cameras. For two guys whose lives were dedicated to capturing proof of the supernatural, it was an amazing experience. For Dierdre, it was a frightening but also validating event. If we could see and hear the activity as well as she could, she wasn't out of her mind as she had feared.

Grant and I had discovered a rare treasure—a woman who could predict what we had always considered unpredictable. How many nights had we spent crawling through attics and closets and basements in people's homes without coming up with a shred of real evidence? How many times had we crisscrossed New England on the off-chance that we would catch a glimpse of the supernatural?

Dierdre's dreams had taken all the guesswork out of ghost-hunting. In her case, it wasn't a matter of *whether* we would encounter paranormal activity. It was only a matter of *when*.

But we couldn't take advantage of her gift—not when we saw the terror on her face at the prospect of reliving her nightmares. If we tried to capitalize on Dierdre's abilities, it would quite possibly be at the expense of her sanity.

In the end, we resisted temptation. We encouraged her to ask the entity that was plaguing her to leave her house. Often, that's all that's necessary to expel a troublesome spirit—a simple, firm request. She did as we asked, but it didn't stop either the dreams or the activity. Stymied, we suggested that she visit her cousin's home by the shore for a couple of weeks to see if the activity continued there.

As it turned out, Dierdre had no supernatural experiences at her cousin's place. In fact, she had no dreams there at all. With that in mind, Grant and I proposed that she try moving to another location. The last we heard from her, she was strongly considering the idea.

Grant: The "Lost" Ghost Hunters Episode

2 0 0 4

You may have heard about our "lost episode." This was the one that never made it to *Ghost Hunters*, the investigation that we set up and videotaped but never put on the air. Well, at long last, this is the story of that case.

First let's set the record straight: A *lot* of our investigations don't make it onto the TV show. In some cases, we find that the place wasn't as interesting as we thought it would be. In other cases, we're expecting complete access to a place and we don't get it. And in still other cases, there's something about the people we meet that makes us think twice about putting them on television.

You can judge for yourself which of these criteria convinced us not to put *this* case on the tube.

Four of us pulled up to the house in rural Maine that

day back in August 2004: Jason, me, an ordained priest named Kevin whom we had worked with several times before, and Steve Gonsalves. Those of you who watch *Ghost Hunters* will recognize Steve's name from the credits, since he's a regular on the show. What you may not know is how far we go back with him.

One day, maybe ten years ago, we got a call from a police officer in western Massachusetts. Apparently, he had heard about T.A.P.S., liked what we stood for, and wanted to join the organization. Unfortunately, he lived two hours away from our headquarters in Warwick, Rhode Island, which was too far, we believed, for him to take part in our group on a regular basis. Our advice to him was to start his own ghost-hunting group instead.

Some time later, we heard about an outfit called New England Paranormal that was doing exceptional work in the area around Springfield, Massachusetts. We contacted them in the hope that we could share techniques and maybe help each other. Much to our surprise, their founder and head honcho was Steve Gonsalves.

From that point on, Steve began to join us on some of our investigations. By the time *Ghost Hunters* hit Syfy he had become a mainstay of our team, though he still remained in charge of his own group back in Springfield.

But none of us, not even Steve, had an idea of what we would find at the home of Mary Alicia Craig. In our first phone conversation with her, which had taken place a couple of weeks earlier, she had said that she was possessed— or at least, she *thought* she was. What she knew for sure was that she was acting strangely.

At T.A.P.S., we don't judge—we investigate. And there

was enough in what Mary Alicia told us to make us suspect some paranormal activity. So we packed up our van and got on the road.

Mary Alicia, it turned out, was in her sixties. Her only companion in the house was her thirty-five-year-old son, Micah, whom she called Junior. He was an odd character, to say the least. In the course of our interview, he made reference over and over again to things he had found in "the diggin' holes"—objects like shoes and bottles and "other stuff"—but he refused to say where these "diggin' holes" might be.

As we walked around the house, we noticed that one of the upstairs bedrooms was padlocked shut. You don't have to be an experienced investigator for a padlock to pique your curiosity. Naturally, we asked the old woman if she would remove the lock and let us get a look inside the room.

"Nothing will be disturbed," I assured the family. "You have my word." And of course, I meant it.

But the son got frantic. No way was he going to let us remove the padlock. That was his stuff in there and no one was going to invade his privacy. Tears started rolling down his cheeks as if he were a child.

It turned out that even the fire department had once been denied access to the room, so it was clear we weren't going to make any headway. Little by little, his mother calmed him down. Only when we were sure Mary Alicia wasn't in any danger did we leave her to take a walk around the property.

On one hand, we were looking for anything, supernatural or otherwise, that might shed light on the family's problems. But we were also taking a moment to share our observations, as we always do at various points in our investigations. We agreed that Mary Alicia and her son had issues, though we weren't entirely convinced that they were of the paranormal variety.

As Jason and I walked, we looked for a sign of the son's "diggin' holes." We couldn't find any. However, we noticed that all of the windows in the building were new except for the one that belonged to the room with the padlock. That one was blacked out. More than ever, we wanted to obtain a look inside.

We decided that, regardless of Junior's resistance, we still had an obligation to help Mary Alicia with her problems. At the least, we could have Kevin cleanse the house through religious provocation. It certainly wouldn't hurt to give it a shot.

Mary Alicia was in favor of the idea, so Kevin got started. Jason and I left him to his work, curious about what Junior was up to. If he had been involved in anything demonic, he would almost certainly react negatively to the ritual. It turned out that we didn't have to go far to find him.

He was right there in the kitchen, doing something by the counter. At first, we couldn't tell what was happening. Then, as we stood there just outside the threshold, we realized that he had pulled up his shirt on one side and was methodically scratching his skin on the sharp corner of the counter.

In fact, he was so intent on what he was doing, he didn't notice us. Deciding not to confront him yet because we didn't want to compromise the ritual, we withdrew into the living room.

Kevin had begun telling the entity to leave, in the name of all that was holy. Mary Alicia was sitting in front of him, nodding. Obviously, she was interested in what he was doing. But she didn't look uncomfortable, much less the way a person looks when a demonic spirit is leaving her body.

Suddenly, Junior erupted into the room, yelping in pain like a dog. His sudden appearance scared the hell out of his mother and interrupted Kevin's pleas. Grimacing, Junior lifted his shirt to show us a series of scratches in the vicinity of his ribs, claiming that he didn't know how they had gotten there.

Jason and I didn't hesitate. We called him on it, saying we had seen him scratch himself on the corner of the kitchen counter. Of course, Junior denied it. He said he had felt some pain, lifted his shirt, and there it was—a claw mark.

Kevin completed the ritual, asking for a sign of the spirit's departure, but it was clear to us that he wasn't getting any results. It wasn't his fault, either. There just wasn't any spirit there in the apartment to exorcise.

Jason sat down on the couch with Mary Alicia and explained why we weren't pleased with the result. "When an inhuman spirit emerges from its host," he told her gently, "you can see it. There's a sign of departure—trembling, shouting, singing, always something along those lines."

She said she thought she had one more spirit in her. "Maybe that's why there wasn't a sign," she suggested.

We asked Kevin if he would repeat the process. With the utmost patience, he went through the ceremony again.

This time, Junior didn't try anything underhanded. He just sat there, watching his mother. When Kevin was done, he again asked for a sign of departure—and Mary Alicia broke into song.

But it wasn't a sign of a spirit departing her body. After having seen dozens of exorcisms, we could tell. There was nothing spontaneous about it, nothing urgent or uncontrollable. It was the kind of singing someone might do if she was trying to give the *impression* a spirit was leaving her.

We had to tell Mary Alicia that we hadn't detected any evidence of a haunting. As far as we could tell, neither she nor her house was beset by ghosts. She accepted the news, but wasn't happy about it. It seemed to us that the idea of a paranormal visitation had created a diversion in her life, which she would miss.

Unprompted, Mary Alicia began to tell us about herself and her family. It turned out that she had two other sons besides Junior, and also a daughter. However, they had all experienced their share of misery. Mary Alicia's daughter and her youngest son had both gotten involved with drug dealers and been murdered as a result. Her daughter had been thrown down a set of stairs and then, as she lay there with a broken neck, shot to death. Her son overdosed and, as his dealer watched, choked to death on his own vomit.

Not the sort of thing you would wish on anyone.

It was a lot for one woman to bear. All things considered, we were surprised she was as stable as she seemed. And if she was looking for a little attention, neither of us could really blame her.

In any case, we had done all we could for Mary Alicia. At least, when it came to the supernatural. The only other thing we could do was give her some practical advice, which no one else might have ever given her.

We told her to clean up the house, bring in some plants, and distance herself from those who caused her emotional pain. Mary Alicia seemed to take the advice to heart. When we left, she seemed to have a new sense of purpose in her life, a new spark of optimism.

As for what was in that locked room that Junior guarded so zealously . . . we will probably never know.

Jason: The Haunted Hotel

2008

The Spalding Inn, a classic New England hotel located in Whitefield, New Hampshire, first started taking in guests way back in the 1860s. It was then that folks from the bustling cities of the Northeast, who wanted to get away for the summer, heard about the great views in New Hampshire's White Mountains and the hospitality of the people who lived there.

The inn was called Cherry Hill House for the first sixty-plus years of its existence. Then, in 1926, it was purchased by Randall and Anna Spalding, who lent the place their family name. The Spaldings had big plans for the hotel, which hadn't changed much since it was expanded in 1865.

Almost immediately they began building the cottages that still stand across the street from the main building, some of which include as many as four bedrooms and four baths, as well as a small kitchen, a living room, a screened porch, and an attic for storage. The Spaldings also built a pool, a number of clay tennis courts, a lawn bowling green, and a pitch-and-putt golf course.

Under its new owners, the inn became a favorite vacation place for well-heeled patrons from Boston, New York, and Montreal. The Spaldings hosted tennis and lawn bowling tournaments that drew people from all over the world, which added to the popularity of their establishment. In fact, they were routinely forced to turn away business in spring, summer, and fall—though never in winter, because the inn was always closed for the colder months.

In the late sixties, the Spaldings took up residence in the house next door to the inn, which was known as the Gray Coach, and turned over the management of their establishment to their two sons. For several years, the brothers ran the inn without incident. Then one of them died on the property, some said by his own hand.

Soon afterward, Anna Spalding died as well. At that point the surviving brother, Donald Spalding, found that his heart was no longer in the business. One thing led to another and the inn went into bankruptcy. It remained closed to the public for many years, while executives of the bank that wound up with it used the place as a private retreat.

The Cockrell family bought the inn in 1991 with intentions of restoring it to its former prominence. It turned out to be an uphill battle, to say the least, as the place had fallen into a state of serious disrepair. The first year the Cockrells ran the inn, they had only four guests—all women in their eighties, who stayed all summer.

However, Mrs. Cockrell was a shrewd businesswoman.

She put together an aggressive marketing campaign, advertising through the *New York Times,* tour bus companies, and wedding brochures. Finally, all her hard work began to bear fruit. The inn started to come alive again.

In fact, it was fully booked for weeks on end. Tour buses stopped for meals there. Sometimes the kitchen was busy preparing dinner for its guests while simultaneously catering a poolside wedding reception. It wasn't unusual for Mrs. Cockrell's daughter, April, to find herself cooking breakfast for forty.

One time April was in the kitchen by herself, preparing the staff meal, when she heard a man's voice say over her shoulder, loud and clear, "What are you doing?" She looked back to see who it was, but there was no one there. At least no one she could see, though she did feel a presence of some kind.

Stunned, but somehow unafraid, April replied that she was making tacos. Then, feeling compelled to explain further, she described the entire procedure from shredding the cheese to cooking the beef. It was only after she finished speaking that she felt the presence fade away.

On another occasion, April was at the inn by herself over the winter. Though the place was closed, she often stayed for weeks at a time to answer the phone. Suddenly, she heard her mother's piano play seven notes.

She could see the piano from where she was sitting, and quite clearly there was no one playing it. But she had heard those seven notes as clear as day. Letting the family dogs out of the office, she took them over to the piano to check it out. However, they didn't appear to sense anything out of the ordinary.

Frightened, April shouted at the top of her lungs, "You are freaking me out and I am here by myself, so please do not do that again!" Whoever or whatever was responsible for those seven notes never played them again—at least not when April was around to hear them.

One autumn, April and her family discovered a stained section of wallpaper in one of the bedrooms. They didn't want to take the time to repaper the entire room when the inn was completely booked, so they figured they would try to replace the stained portion first. After all, they had dozens of rolls of wallpaper up in their attics. One of them was bound to match the bedroom in question.

Just their luck, they couldn't find any paper that matched. At that point, they decided to wait until spring and repaper the entire room. As busy as they were, it was really the only other option.

But in the spring, when they went up to one of the attics to find new paper for the room, they found something on the attic stairs—five complete rolls of the paper they had been looking for six months earlier. And each one was wrapped with a bow. Other items in demand at the hotel showed up the same way—months later, wrapped with a bow.

It got to the point where the Cockrells stopped looking for things they needed. They just wished for them out loud, hoping they would turn up a few months later. And the family was seldom disappointed.

One of the ghosts in the place, according to April, is the spirit of Anna Spalding. It's said that she'll play the piano if it's put in a certain place in the living room. While she was still alive, she used to sit there in the evenings and play for the benefit of the guests down the hall.

The spirit of Mrs. Fairchild, whose family owned Fairchild Publications, is another that supposedly haunts the inn. Mrs. Fairchild would come up from New York to spend the summers there. April herself took the woman to get her hair done every Tuesday at ten in the morning, then went back and picked her up around noon.

April told us that her mother saw Mrs. Fairchild's ghost for the first time on a snowy day in midwinter. During the cold months, the Cockrells used to occupy the six rooms located above the family room, so they made use of the driveway out front. One day, shortly after Mrs. Fairchild's death, April's mother drove up the driveway and saw the woman sitting on the passenger side of April's car—as if she were waiting for her regular ride to the hairdresser.

In 2000, April's dad was diagnosed with cancer, and Mrs. Cockrell put the inn up for sale. In 2003, the family sold the property and moved back to Buffalo, New York, where they were from originally. After that, the property went through more than one pair of hands, none of them making a go of it.

Grant and I were told about the inn by a friend who knew the current owner. He mentioned it to us because it was reputed to be haunted, though no one had ever attempted to verify the rumors. I guess he thought that T.A.P.S. might want to investigate the place.

My partner and I had other ideas. For the longest time, we had dreamed of buying a haunted establishment of some kind. We had been in any number of them in the course of our investigations, and we had always envied their proprietors a little bit. This was an opportunity for us to become proprietors ourselves.

We called the owner and talked to him. As it happened, he was wide open to the idea of selling us the inn. However, we needed to see the place before we took the conversation any further.

The owner allowed us to stay at the inn for two nights by ourselves, so we could see what it was like. This wasn't intended to be a formal investigation of the place by any means. We didn't bring cameras, audio recorders, EMF meters, or the rest of our equipment. We were just going to sleep there for a couple of nights to get a sense of what we might be getting ourselves into.

As it got dark outside and we settled into our rooms, we wondered what we were going to encounter. Maybe nothing, despite what we had been told about the place. It wouldn't be the first time we had heard impressive claims and failed to uncover any significant paranormal activity.

Nothing happened for a good few hours. Then, as the time approached midnight, Grant and I heard the sound of footsteps coming from the floor above us. We went upstairs to check them out, but there was no one there. We looked at each other.

"We both heard those footsteps," I said. "And we're supposed to be alone here. That was the deal, wasn't it?"

Grant nodded. "Let's go back downstairs and see if we hear them again."

We didn't. But we heard something else—a kind of whispering. We walked around the inn, trying to find its source, but couldn't come up with anything. Finally we gave up and went back to our rooms.

On the way, we passed the front desk. Grant and I were still talking about the whispering we'd heard, so I wasn't as alert as I might have been. Still, I caught a glimpse of something unusual.

A shadow, behind the front desk. The shadow of a *person*, as far as I could tell. And it wasn't staying in one place. It was moving around, from side to side. But there didn't seem to be anyone projecting it.

As I pointed in an attempt to get Grant's attention, I realized he was doing the same thing. But before either of us could say anything, the shadow faded. A moment later, it vanished altogether.

"That was interesting," I said.

"Sure was," said my partner.

We checked to make sure there was no one in the vicinity of the desk who could have cast the shadow. There wasn't. Not a soul.

The next night, we heard the footsteps again. And as before, we couldn't find anyone who might be making them. We also heard the whispering, and couldn't come up with an explanation for that either.

We hadn't conducted a proper investigation of the inn, but then we didn't have to. There wasn't any client depending on us to tell him if the place was haunted. There was only us, trying to figure out if the stories about the inn might be true.

And we came to the conclusion that they were.

The result? The two of us called the owner and told him we wanted to buy the place. We closed on the property on October 8, 2008, and haven't looked back. In fact, the inn has turned out to be a treasure trove of supernatural occurrences. The more Grant and I have occasion to stay there with our families, the more experiences we have.

For instance, Grant and his wife, Reanna, were walking through the lobby area after dusk one evening when they distinctly heard a man's voice say something to them. But there was no one else present in the lobby. So who spoke to them?

Later that same night, Grant's mother-in-law was lying on the couch in the lobby when she noticed a shadow moving around behind the front desk. No person, just a shadow. Later, she described it to us as something moving from side to side, which was pretty much what Grant and I had experienced the first night we were there.

But in our case, the shadow vanished a moment after we caught sight of it. Grant's mother-in-law was able to watch it for a while. It only began to fade when she got up to tell us about it.

Even later, my wife, Kristen, and I were finally starting to fall asleep when we heard a long, high-pitched scream. Our first thought was that someone—either in Grant's family or in mine—had gotten hurt and needed help. But when we checked, we found everyone was all right.

The next day, in the hallway on the second floor of the main house, Reanna was going back to her room for something when she felt something grab her leg. At first, she thought it was one of the kids playing a trick on her. Then she realized that she was alone in the hallway.

Grant's son Connor, who is all of ten years old, had an experience as well. He was walking through the kitchen when he felt something touch him. Like Reanna, he thought someone was kidding around with him and went looking for the jokester. However, the kitchen was empty except for him. When he mentioned the incident to the rest of us, we added it to the inn's rapidly growing list of unexplained phenomena.

Early that afternoon, Reanna and Connor were standing in the restaurant, looking out at the carriage house, and saw a woman in one of the upstairs windows. That was enough to send chills up their spines, because the place was supposed to be empty except for our families. Then they realized that the woman was looking back at them.

Before they could say anything, she turned and walked out of sight. Reanna brought it to our attention and we went upstairs to see who might be up there. After an exhaustive search, we concluded that the house was unoccupied.

My daughter Haily couldn't quite accept that. She decided to inspect the place on her own. When she did, she caught a glimpse of a shadow. It disappeared after a moment, but not before Haily fixed it in her mind.

We asked her about it afterward, thinking there might be a connection between the woman and the shadow. Haily couldn't say for sure that it was the shadow of a woman. On the other hand, she couldn't say it *wasn't*.

Overall, we thoroughly enjoyed our stay at the inn. None of the activity that came our way was so scary as to make us uncomfortable, and we all loved the idea that there were mysteries waiting to be pursued. Far from being frightened, our kids keep asking us when we're going up for another visit.

Our executive chef, Slayton, has had some experiences of his own. He has seen shadowy heads peeking around corners and then vanishing when he pursues them in the hope of identifying them. He has also heard voices in the hallway late at night. Yet when he takes a look around, he never sees anyone.

Given the amount of activity we've all experienced at the inn, and its long history of ghostly goings-on, Grant and I have decided to have the place investigated. Just one problem—we can't do it ourselves. There's a saying that anyone who serves as his own lawyer in court has a fool for a client. We think it applies to ghost-hunting as well. Remember, an investigator needs to approach a case in as unbiased a manner as possible, and Grant and I, as the owners of the place, are definitely biased.

So we've engaged the services of another investigative outfit, one for which we have the utmost respect. In a matter of weeks from the time of this writing, the Spalding Inn will play host to the team from *Ghost Hunters International*.

It'll be weird for Grant and me to be on the other side of the fence, in the role of the client instead of the investigator. We expect to learn a few things from the experience, which will no doubt serve us in good stead in the future. After all, it's one thing to anticipate how a client will feel when a ghost-hunting group shows up, and another to actually be in the client's shoes.

Also, our claims will be in the hands of *GHI* to verify, and not in our own. That'll be a little frustrating. The investigator in us will make us want to roll up our sleeves and pitch in, and it'll take a fair amount of willpower to keep from doing so.

On the other hand, Grant and I can look forward to hearing their findings. That'll be fun. And not just for us, because when the investigation is over, it will be shown to the viewing public as an episode of *Ghost Hunters International*.

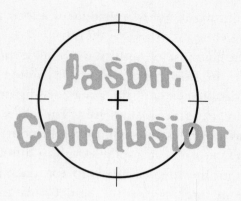

Jason: Conclusion

So now you know how it was back then, before we ever imagined we would be signing up for our sixth season of hunting ghosts on Syfy. In a lot of ways, things have changed. For instance, we have access to equipment we could only have dreamed about when we started out. And we don't have to go over the data we've collected in a basement, the way we used to. But in all the ways that matter, things are exactly the same.

For instance, we're still as devoted as ever to our families back in Rhode Island. That's a priority for us and it always will be. We've seen all kinds of husbands and fathers, good and bad, in our line of work, so we know how important it is to make time for our wives and kids.

Also, we still work as plumbers for Roto-Rooter, the largest provider of plumbing and drain-cleaning services in North America. Shortly after Grant and I met at that doughnut shop, I took him away from his job as a systems administrator for a major manufacturing company and put him in plumber's overalls. After all, I needed a partner, and he seemed like a guy I wouldn't want to kill after a couple of jobs.

Another aspect of our lives that hasn't changed is our passion for investigation. We're still bound and determined to make the field of paranormal inquiry more scientifically acceptable. That's why we're constantly reining in our investigators, asking them to back up their claims with solid proof.

One thing that always surprises us is the caliber of the places we get to investigate. The *Queen Mary*, for instance, arguably the most famous ship in the world. Or the elegant Stanley Hotel in Colorado, where they filmed the Stephen King movie *The Shining*. Or the cavernous Eastern State Penitentiary in Philadelphia, where Al Capone went out of his mind.

How about Myrtle's Plantation in Louisiana, known far and wide as "the most haunted place in America"? Or Leap Castle in Ireland, home to a demon summoned centuries ago with the help of the dark arts? Or St. Augustine Lighthouse in Florida, where we chased a spook up hundreds of feet of stairs?

All amazing venues. All challenging, each in a different way. And all beyond our wildest dreams when we were taking on our earliest cases in unassuming little hamlets all over New England.

Funny thing, though . . . with all the places we've been and the magnitude of the investigations we've carried out, we still get the biggest jolt out of poking through someone's dark, dusty closet, or listening for voices in a damp basement at four in the morning. Underneath it all, that's still us. It's where our hearts are and, we expect, where they'll always be.

Because that's where you find the people. The ones who look to us with panic in their eyes, hoping we can find them some answers. The ones who don't know how they'll protect their children from something they don't understand.

Even now, we often put our clients' needs ahead of our own, whether they want a demon expelled, a waste pipe welded, or just a hand to hold. After all, they're the reason we got into this field in the first place. And having been in their shoes at one time, we know exactly how they feel.

Really, when you come right down to it, ghost-hunting isn't about the ghosts so much. It's not about the dead. It's about the living.

And if we're lucky, we'll do more than help the people who contact us. We'll also expand our knowledge of paranormal phenomena. It won't be easy, with all the obstacles we have to overcome in even the simplest investigations. But hey, if we keep plugging away, who knows?

Stranger things have happened.

It's been a great adventure, this excursion into the realm of the supernatural that started so many years ago. We consider it a privilege, one that few people ever get an opportunity to experience. And we're glad that you, the reader, were able to come along for part of the ride.

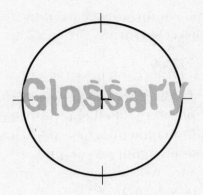

Glossary

APPARITION

A disembodied spirit visible to human beings.

ASTRAL PLANE

A level of existence separate from and in some sense higher than the physical world, according to certain philosophies and religious teachings.

COLD SPOT

A place that is cooler than the surrounding area. It is thought by some to be an indication of a supernatural presence draw-ing energy from its environment in order to manifest.

COUPLING

Using other forms of investigative documentation in conjunction with photography to create more com-pelling evidence of paranormal activity. For instance, using an audio recorder to capture EVPs whenever a particular image appears.

DIGITAL INFRARED CAMERA

A device used to capture images invisible to the human eye at the "hot" end of the light spectrum. It is capable of feeding information to a computer, where its infrared images may be stored on a hard drive.

DIGITAL THERMOMETER

A device used to record the presence of "cold spots" and "hot spots," sometimes during an apparent paranormal event. Some digital thermometers record temperatures second by second for PC storage and graphic charting.

ECTOPLASM

A filmy, quasisolid substance that supposedly issues from the bodies of mediums while they are in trance states. Ectoplasm may issue from the mouth, the nostrils, the eyes, the ears, the navel, or the nipples. In photographs, ectoplasm resembles muslin fabric soaked in water.

ELECTROMAGNETIC FIELD RECORDER

A device used to record data on electromagnetic fields (EMFs). Its use is controversial among ghost hunters in that EMFs from power lines, television sets, kitchen applicances, and so forth surround us constantly, and it has yet to be categorically proven that ghosts emit EM energy. On the other hand, some researchers say ghosts disrupt EMFs.

EVP
Electronic voice phenomena. Audio devices may record disembodied voices and other supernatural sounds that are not directly audible to the human ear.

EXORCISM
Ritual expulsion of invading spiritual or demonic entities from a person or dwelling. The term was brought into the common vernacular by the 1973 movie *The Exorcist*.

FLOATING ORB
A spherical image, usually a translucent white though sometimes a reddish or bluish hue, which inexplicably registers on film or videotape. Its presence is thought by some to be an indicator of supernatural activity.

GHOST
The soul or spirit of a dead person, reflecting the appearance of his or her living body but less substantial. Ghosts may exist in a state of semiawareness or be completely cognizant of their living observers.

GHOST HUNTER/INVESTIGATOR
A person who attempts to gather evidence of ghosts or other paranormal activity. This may be accomplished by

means of still photography, video, audio, EMF recordings, EVP recordings, or other means.

GLOBULE

A ball of light, often seen in groups, that is visible to the naked eye. Its presence is believed to be an indicator of paranormal activity.

HAUNTING

The manifestation of a ghostly presence attached to a specific person or location.

INCUBUS

A male demon who lies on top of women as they sleep in order to have sexual intercourse with them.

INHUMAN ENTITY

A demon or other spirit intent on causing harm to living beings. Also known as a negative entity or a demonic entity.

INTELLIGENT HAUNTING

A supernatural entity that is aware of its surroundings and/or observers and is capable of interacting with them.

MATERIALIZATION

The procedure through which a ghost appears. Materialization can be sudden or gradual, resulting in an entity that is indistinct or seemingly quite solid.

MATRIXING

The natural tendency of the human mind to add details to sensory input (perceived through the visual, auditory, olfactory, or tactile senses) so as to create a familiar or easily understood pattern. In effect, matrixing is mentally "filling in the blanks."

NEGATIVE ENTITY

(See "Inhuman entity.")

OUIJA BOARD

A wooden board preprinted with letters, numbers, and words, used by mediums to receive supernatural communications.

PARANORMAL

The realm of occurrences and phenomena removed from those to which people are exposed in everyday experience.

PHANTOM SMELL

Any scent through which a supernatural entity is attempting to express itself. Typically, phantom smells are reminiscent of flowers, cigarettes, or perfume, but they don't come from any identifiable source.

POLTERGEIST

A ghost that manifests its presence through noises, rappings, the moving of objects, and the creation of disorder. The relocation of furniture is an indication of poltergeist activity.

POSSESSION

A situation in which a hostile spirit enters and takes control of a human body, causing noticeable changes in behavior.

RELIGIOUS PROVOCATION

The use of prayer, holy water, and/or religious artifacts to make an inhuman entity show itself and leave a location. Only those trained in this kind of ritual should consider employing it.

RESIDUAL HAUNTING

A scene from the past that continues to be played out over and over again, like a recording, with the witness of the phenomenon essentially peering into a former era. The ghostly participants in these time displacements often seem unaware of their living observers.

SENSITIVE

A medium, psychic, or clairvoyant. A sensitive can see or feel people, objects, and events in the realm of the paranormal.

THERMAL IMAGING DIGITAL CAMERA

A device that records images of long-wavelength infrared radiation (that is, heat) that are invisible to the human eye. The thermal imaging camera facilitates the capture of images in darkness, smoke, or fog.

VORTEX

An anomaly that sometimes shows up in still photographs taken at the site of a suspected haunting, appearing as a translucent white tube or funnel-shaped mass. Some researchers believe vortices may be portals to the spirit realm.